NIGHT IN OUR VEINS

Paul Edwards

NIGHT IN OUR VEINS

GRAVESTONE PRESS

DEDICATION

Dedicated to John B. Ford and to the memory of
Steve Lines

6

LEITMOTIF

*"Sounds – possibly musical – heard in the
night from other worlds or realms of being."*
- H.P. Lovecraft

Viktor was woken by the sound of soft, sweet music.

He lay there listening, hands clasped across his chest, fingers intertwined.

The music filled his head with an assortment of images:

Magic circles chalked on stripped bare floorboards. Scattered scraps of hand drawn sheet music. A photograph of a smiling couple in a frame propped up on the lid of a grand piano. A dusty bookcase crammed with esoteric tomes and crumbling grimoires.

Darkness tugged at the corners of his vision. He was having trouble keeping his eyes open. Sleep was pulling him back in its full embrace. But the music was haunting, almost impossible to tune out of, its magic brushing away his lethargy and suffusing him with joy.

His arms dropped to his sides, his fingers lightly tapping the base of the bed. The music, he realised, was coming from a lone violin. This unlocked precious memories within him, each one startlingly vivid and emotional in detail.

They helped draw him to his feet at last, the bones in his body popping. He edged across the room, pressing his hands up against the door. The door yielded, creaking quietly open.

Beyond the door stood a woman, her eyelids fluttering, a baroque violin tucked under her chin. Moonlight glinted off the necklace she wore: a large silver pentacle attached to a chain. Long black hair with grey roots fell about her face as she shimmied and swayed, a discarded padlock lying on the ground between her feet.

She lifted her head, catching his gaze.

Immediately, her eyes widened.

Her jaw dropped.

She played on, the melody painting the night and the insides of his skull with wonder.

She was smiling and crying, all at the same time.

And then he remembered.

It was *his* song.

The song Ilse had written.

Ilse, he thought; *of course!*

The song that spoke of a special bond, stronger than any obstacle, than any adversary. And *he* was the song – it was part of his essence, his very being intertwined with the sparse, ghostly refrain.

Her black lace dress swished about her ankles, tears leaking down her aged but still breathtakingly beautiful face.

When the music stops, he thought, *sleep will steal me from the world once more.*

But for now, he remained entranced in the doorway of his small stone house, watching,

8

listening to her play his song amongst the crosses and headstones of the garden.

Where The Wounded Trees Wait

Dedicated to the memory of William "Billy"
Edwards
11/11/1908 – 31/08/1991

Introduction

Iesu! Cyfaill f'enaid cu!

Iesu, cyfaill f'enaid cu,
I dy fynwes gad im' ffoi.
Tra bo'r dyfroedd o bob tu,
A'r ym tymhestloedd yn crynhoi.
Cudd fi, O fy Mhrynwr! cudd,
Nes 'r el heibio'r storom gref;
Yn arweinydd imi bydd
Nes im' dd'od i dyernas nef.
Noddfa arall gwn nid oes,
Ond Tydi i'm henaid gwan;
Ti, fu farw ar a groes
Yw fy nghymorth yn mhob man;
Ynot, O fy Iesu! mae
Holl ymddiried f'enaid byw:
nerth rho imi i barhau,
Nes dod adref, at fy Nuw.
Pob peth ynot, Iesu, mae;
Mwy na phopeth ynot sydd;
Cyfod Di'r syrthiedig rai,
Ac i'r cleifion meddyg bydd;

I'r gwangalon cysur rho,
Deillion tywys yn dy ffyrdd;
Ninnau yn dragyddol rown
Ar dy ben fendithion fyrdd.
Gras sydd ynot fel y mor,
Gras i faddeu fy holl fai;
Boed i'w ffrydiau, Arglwydd Iôr!
Oddi wrth bechod fy nglanhau;
Ffynnon bywyd f'enaid gwiw,
Rhydd im' gysur ar fy nhaith,
Llona f'ysbryd tra b'wyf byw,
Tardd i dragwyddoldeb maith!

(Welsh soldiers sang 'Jesus, Lover Of My Soul' to composer Joseph Parry's tune, 'Aberystwyth', before going into battle at Mametz in 1916. The words represent a deep, heartfelt calling on God to provide, if not protection physically, then at least the courage to face whatever may lie ahead.)

***

"You have it…" the old woman reached out, touching the crown of the child's head, "…but don't be frightened – it's a gift! That's what your grandfather believed, anyway." She took her hand away, tilting her head to the side and smiling. "I've only been able to look back. Perhaps it's the same for you… although it's more than scrying, remember? And it's important to talk; not to brush it under the carpet and pretend it's not there. What hope do we have if we don't talk about it, if we don't try and understand?"

Her fingers brushed the child's face, as light as feathers. "When I was your age," she said, "I couldn't read a book without having to scan the last few pages first. I had to be sure there was a happy ending, see." She shook her head, chuckled to herself. "But I've learnt to let the future be." Her eyes clouded suddenly and for a moment or two she was miles away, locked in some other world, some other time completely. Then, blinking twice, refocusing, added: "I think I knew, in my heart of hearts, what would happen. Perhaps I should have tried harder... Maybe there could have been some way of...preventing it." A deep frown joined her eyebrows together. "But whenever I scry, I discern loops and terrible dark patterns..."

Her fingers slipped away from the child, and a powerful silence enfolded them both.

The child gazed at the woman's troubled expression, no longer feeling quite so alone.

Chapter I

She walked barefoot toward the gaunt skeletons of the trees. Mud splashed and squelched, squishing up between her toes, spattering the backs of her legs. All around the land was an eerie nightscape of smoking craters, dead bodies, broken picket posts and barbed wire. Some men, still alive, mortally wounded, were crying out and begging for water. Some plucked at her legs as she went by.

In blasted shell holes she saw men who'd had limbs blown off and others who, having been shot, had crawled in from the machine gun fire to die. She scanned each face, looking for him, but couldn't make him out, couldn't see him yet.

Horror and frustration threatened to overwhelm her. A fusilier with half his head blown away lay against his machine gun, hand still on the trigger. Another was kneeling close to the wood, a red trickle creeping from his bayonetted throat. To her left, a young man was running in wild circles, shrieking, his mind clearly broken by war.

The wood loomed, all light shrinking away suddenly, unnaturally. The trees were calling for her, she thought. Beckoning her in. Wanting her for their own. "We gravitate together," she breathed. "It's what we do."

Lumps of flesh hung over branches like discoloured rags. Decapitated heads gazed up with

13

glassy, soulless eyes. A human hand crouched in a bisected tree trunk like a pale grotesque spider.

Then the trees were moving, waving in a strange, hypnotic fashion, their branches reaching down slowly, mesmerizingly, enfolding her like they were arms, holding her close, still and tight. In the blink of an eye they were arms – sinewy and stripped of flesh, dripping blood on the leaves and twigs scattered around her.

She closed her eyes as they eased her to the ground, a weird sense of serenity descending as she hugged them back, easing her racing heart and reeling mind.

And then, for the first time since she could remember, before she would wake up, choking and gasping, she felt at peace, whole.

***

I do not want to die out here alone…

Huw's words ghosted through Caryl's head as she sat patiently at the table, eyes fastened on the clock on the wall. She felt unusually calm, focused and ready for scrying.

Gene's hand slid into his pocket, fidgeting with an object. His gaze drifted from her face, fixing itself on some indeterminable spot above her shoulder.

"How will you…? he began, then dropped his gaze to his knees, pensive and silent. Moments later, he looked up and tried again. "Do you know exactly…?" He shook his head, defeated.

The waiter came over with a bottle of Côtes du Rhône, showing Caryl the label. He uncorked it, poured a small amount into Caryl's glass.

She sipped. "C'est bon."

"Aimez-vous?"

"Oui, c'est très bien."

The waiter smiled, nodded and filled their glasses before moving on to the next table.

Caryl ran a finger around the rim of her wine glass. "I'm here. We're actually here, Gene."

The crimson light of the swiftly setting sun trailed through the windows, spilling slanted beams across the table top and floor.

"I'm glad you came," she said, reaching out, stroking his knuckles. "I didn't think you would."

It was a conscious change of tack. She'd grown increasingly aware over the past few days that she'd been irritable and dismissive of him. Anxiety had been bubbling up, clawing for release.

"It is pretty here," Gene conceded. "Quiet, though. Perhaps a little too quiet for my taste."

She knew he had an agenda; business of his own. He was waiting for the right time to broach it, she supposed. Whatever it was that he wanted to say, she hoped he wouldn't raise it here, at the table, because all she wanted to talk about was scrying.

Fleetingly she thought of Jake and how he'd talk incessantly and passionately about everything and anything, it seemed. They were chalk and cheese, Gene and Jake. Couldn't be more different if they tried.

A week ago, she'd slept with Jake again. She'd promised herself that she wouldn't do it, but she fell

15

under his spell and spent the night at his. In his bed, he'd made the usual idle promises, whilst listing reasons why her relationship with Gene would fail.

The waiter reappeared, setting their main courses down in front of them.

"The battlefield's about a mile from here." She threw a hopeful glance at Gene. "Perhaps we could go for a walk after supper?"

"Must be like looking for a needle in a haystack."

"Think I've pinpointed it, thanks to Nan's efforts over the years."

Gene thanked the departing waiter, then puffed out his cheeks and sighed.

What did this mean to him, if anything, she wondered? Could he imagine himself here, seventy-two years ago, crouched in a trench, miles from home and knowing that he could die, at any given moment, far from everyone and everything he loved?

She set her cutlery down, reached under the table for her rucksack and opened it. Maybe this would make it real, she thought, taking out the photograph, passing it to him.

He put his fork down and studied the photograph.

She knew the picture like the back of her hand. Huw, in his 1902 Pattern Service Dress tunic, trousers and hat. He'd a kind, compassionate face and eyes that seemed to convey a message which she couldn't quite decipher.

The photo was old and brittle. The thought of it perishing someday distressed her. "I think you look like your Nan," he said, handing the photograph back. "You, your Mum; your Nan. You all look the same." He picked his fork back up and resumed eating. "You should smile more, Caryl. I never see you smile."

She pretended not to hear him.

Leaning across the table, teeth bared, she said, "I can find him. I know I can."

***

Excerpt from the diary of Pte Huw Price: -

6th December 1915

We set off just before five, after the carts and horses had boarded. There had been torrential rain in Southampton, so I was soaked through by the time I arrived at my berthing space on the boat.

It did not take long to find my bed – bunk numbers correspond with the number written on your billet, which is issued as you board. The bunk is comfortable enough, consisting of a strip of canvas supported by four iron uprights. At least I have a bed; some fellows here have had to make do with the floor, as there are not enough bunks to go round.

The washroom is located opposite and, as I was picking my way across the sleeping men earlier, the sway of the boat knocked me on top of one chap who made the most dreadful fuss. I apologised profusely, picked myself up and made my way to the washroom before he could wake the entire boat up.

It goes without saying that I am missing you and Sara, Siân. I am surrounded by people, yet I have never felt more alone in my life. It has made me realise how much I take for granted, and how lucky I am to have you both.

Before I left, do you remember what we talked about? That conversation we had about your gift? I firmly believe it is a gift. In fact, I envy your talent and ability to think and feel as deeply as you do.

They say you cannot know another person but believe me when I say that what I feel for you is both strong and true. You are never far from my thoughts. Sara, too. You give me purpose, a reason to live. I carry you both in my heart, no matter where I go.

Chapter II

Caryl gazed up at the dragon, which faced the wood and was tearing at barbed wire. She ran her fingers across the words carved on the plinth – MAMETZ WOOD – and sang, softly, "Llona f'ysbryd tra b'wyf byw, tardd i dragwyddoldeb maith." It was the hymn that the soldiers had sung shortly before advancing; Jesus, Lover Of My Soul to the tune of Aberystwyth.

Gene touched her elbow. She flicked open her eyes and whispered, "Think I've been here before."

Gene backed away, shoulders hunched, face in shadow, toward the information plaque opposite the sculpture. Does he know more than he lets on, she wondered? Would he dash her head against the plinth in a jealous rage?

"Which battalion was your grandfather in?" he called suddenly, a disembodied voice in the darkness.

"He was in the 16th Battalion, under the 115th Brigade." She edged toward him, mud squelching and sucking at her shoes. "A two-pronged simultaneous assault." She tucked a loose strand of hair behind her ear, then added: "Once they entered the wood, both Divisions were to advance towards the centre ride and then swing to the north, clearing the enemy as they advanced." She squinted at the plaque as she continued, "The 38th had the added task of sweeping across the southern end to clear any enemy from that locality."

"They suffered catastrophic casualties."

19

"More than 400 men." White mist escaped her lips, wheeling, curling in on itself. "Grandad hung on in there. Lasted until nightfall; around this time, I suppose."

"Where did they attack?"

She waved a pale hand and said, "There, to the south-east. Got as far as 200 yards."

They trudged down metal steps then started across the field together. Overhead, ragged clouds drifted across a waxing moon.

"Huw was last seen by Private Davies a couple of hundred yards from the wood." She pointed at the stark-black trees ahead, standing like sentries in the night. "He dug in, sheltering from the intense shelling and gunfire." She glanced around at the dragon, which was now just a shadow on the hilltop. "One of the last of the 115th to fall."

He nodded once but didn't reply. She'd hoped that he'd put an arm around her, or take her hand; instead, he kept his head bowed, his gaze lowered as they traipsed solemnly toward the wood.

"Around here…" She stopped suddenly, dropping her rucksack. "…he sheltered from the bombardment in a shell hole. Dug right in and held his position."

She opened her rucksack and took out Huw's diary; a jewellery box; photographs; Davies' letters. Sat quietly beside them, studying them in turn.

Gene hitched his jeans up and dropped to his haunches. "Is that everything?"

"Everything I can use." Her gaze drifted over Davies' words, a soldier who'd survived Mametz and had documented his experiences in letters to

20

loved ones back home. Huw was mentioned, as well as other men from the 38th (Welsh) Infantry Division. Davies had described Huw's immense bravery and courage, fighting back in a shell hole before succumbing at the edge of the wood at around 2100 hours.

There were more photographs tucked inside the diary, taken by Caryl's grandmother. Each depicted the spot where they now sat, although the pictures were of the wood and field in broad daylight.

"Nan came out here in '79, '81 and '85," Caryl explained. "These were taken three years ago, in '85; the year before Nan died. Huw's diary, the letters... they helped Nan pinpoint where it was he perished."

Gene was hunched deep into his coat, hands thrust in his pockets. "How long do you think it'll take?"

"Could be a night. Maybe two. Could be a week. But I don't want to leave until..."

"Just be careful, okay? I know how it devastates you. I remember after your grandmother..." He trailed off, not needing to continue. She felt his eyes on her but couldn't meet them. Didn't need his concern now.

She examined a photograph of Huw and Siân on their wedding day, Siân dressed in a satin gown and veil; a photograph of Huw with Mum in his lap when Mum had been a baby; the picture of Huw in his full Service Dress, a hint of a smile etching his youthful face.

She touched the letters, her fingers careful not to damage those faded, brittle leaves. Closed her

21

eyes and repeated a line from Huw's diary: "I carry you both in my heart, no matter where I go."

She opened the jewellery box, took out a lock of his hair. Nan had cut it from her husband's head just before he'd left and now, holding it up, Caryl whispered and chanted strange, esoteric words. She closed her eyes, a rushing sound filling her skull. When she opened them again, the world flickered and jumped like a trapped frame on a screen.

Keep concentrating, she thought. Keep chanting; focusing...

From the distance came the sounds of detonation; the barking of orders, warnings and commands. She kept her wide-open eyes nailed to the moon, specks dancing across her vision, flashing, jumping, flickering. She had to utilise all her senses to bring forth the past, to transport herself to where she needed to go...

She suddenly began to tremble, then her body shook in a spectacular spasm. If Gene intervened now, she'd hate him, particularly after everything she'd instructed, after everything she'd...

Her head rolled and the moon tumbled – a sickening white blur – and there was a hole now, a portal; a tear in reality – opening, widening; whiteness burning like a supernova at the edges of her vision...

She saw holes in the trees and flames licking around trunks. Heard shrieks and saw people – shadowy blurs – flit past and through her as she focused on anchoring herself, of solidifying herself at the scene. All around the air was filling with the rattle of machine guns and the screams of the dying.

Shells howled overhead, the ground rocking beneath her feet as they exploded nearby.

There – dug into the earth not far from the wood – a collection of twisting, writhing bodies squirming through smoke… Could one be…?

The light was suddenly like a burning magnesium ribbon – and then she was back to herself, back in darkness, silence, huddled over, gasping, panting, wheezing at the ground.

Gene laid his hand on her shoulder. "Are you…?"

She vomited and he withdrew his hand quickly.

He grabbed a packet of tissues from her rucksack, dabbed the sick around her mouth. Her nose was bleeding so he cleaned that up, too. Then he scooped Siân's items up, carefully packing them back into the rucksack. "Can you walk?"

Caryl nodded desolately, got up and they trudged across the field together, back toward Mametz. She was sick once more in the hotel, retching into the toilet in their bathroom. She scraped her hair away from her face, straightened. Stared long and hard into the mirror above the sink. She was so thin; skeletal, almost. Fluorescent lighting washed over the criss-cross of self-inflicted scars on her arms. She felt Gene's eyes on them but didn't care.

"You okay?"

She padded into the room, then sat beside him on the bed. Lowering her head, she pinched tissue out of her nostrils and placed the bloodied, squashed-up balls on the bedside table.

Downstairs, a Frenchman began talking to someone; then a door closed loudly, firmly, causing silence to settle once more.

"Do you think you'll be sick again?" he asked.

"Don't think so." She laughed without humour. "Can't imagine there's much left to come out." She glanced at him. "I was close, Gene. I was right back there, you know?"

When he didn't reply, she turned on him: "Why the hell do I talk to you about it? You don't believe in anything you can't see, right?"

"Yes, I don't understand!" He was shaking now, his eyes wide, round, and blazing. "But I'm here, aren't I? Isn't that enough?"

She shook her head, wishing it was Jake here. But that could never happen, because Jake wouldn't commit. Had never shown the slightest inclination of settling down. Besides, she'd hate for him to see her like this.

She held up her trembling arms, gaze dancing over the scars on her flesh. "I don't deserve to be here."

"Caryl…"

"Let me finish." She fixed him with a glare. "I mean, what am I? Really? What have I achieved?" She mumbled to herself, drawing the back of her hand across her eyes. "It's the guilt that eats me, you know? I'm a fucking waste of time and space. That's why this is important – I've got to give something back." Her hands dropped limply in her lap, her fingers flexing, furling. "It's the living that scares me, Gene."

24

"I know." He gripped her shoulder, then squeezed. "But I think this brings you down. It's a curse..." he trailed off, seemingly unsure as to whether to continue or not.

She sat dead still, mulling over his words.

"I think you need to rest," he said at last. "You'll feel better in the morning."

"Don't fucking patronise me."

"I'm not..."

She shot up, walked to the other side of the bed and dragged back the duvet. Crawled into bed and pressed herself against the wall with her back to him, silent and still. He groaned, undressed and climbed into bed with her.

His arm hesitantly snaked around her body to squeeze and hold her tight. It was the first time he'd held her since they'd arrived. She thought about the last thing Jake had said, in a café before she'd gone to France: "We'll come back to each other. We gravitate together, it's what we do."

She twisted onto her back, lost herself to silence. Soon, Gene began to snore. She stared at the ceiling, feeling empty, a melee of thoughts churning in her mind...

Thick, smoggy darkness descended.

Out of the darkness came hollered orders, warnings and commands.

The wood loomed, flashing a deep, ominous red. Tongues of flame flickered between tree trunks. Severed heads and lumps of flesh hung in the claws of splintered branches. Mangled corpses in khaki and field grey lay in a smouldering crater, frightfully mutilated, one lad decapitated by a shell, just as if he'd been guillotined. Everywhere the ground was littered with broken guns, bayonets, shells and men.

Smoke poured forth from the trees, fierce and black, almost obscuring all vision, its acrid stench filling Caryl's nostrils and clawing at her throat. Struggling to breathe, to see, she tried to focus on a man who'd turned briefly, fleetingly, in her direction.

Realisation hit her…

She staggered forwards, shouting and shrieking Huw's name.

Machine guns roared.

Screams erupted.

Shells whistled.

She was almost in arm's reach, but still he didn't turn; still didn't react. Smoke drove into her eyes, blinding her. Then, seeing him again, she grit her teeth and ploughed on, almost falling, tripping, arm outstretched, fingers moving…

"Caryl!"

Gene was leaning over her, his eyes bulging white circles in the shadows across his face. "Caryl, you okay?" His voice quietened, softened. "You were crying out in your sleep again."

She barely heard his words, his voice. Her hand slipped from his shoulder and she rolled over, away from him, choking and weeping bitter tears until sleep claimed her once more.

***

26

Excerpts from the diary of Pte Huw Price: -

30th December 1915

It has not stopped raining for two days straight. The trenches are ankle deep – some places calf deep – in mud and in other places there are rushing streams of foul-smelling brown water.

We spend most of our time displacing the mud, either by filling sandbags or piling it up into a wall and beating it into a firm rampart.

Rats surround us – last night they were all over me, scrabbling after the rations in my haversack. When they scurried close to my face, I leapt up, cursing and spitting, searching the trench for another spot to lie down in.

The days bleed into each other and nothing seems to change. Fear, boredom, boredom, fear – they swing from one to another and we are all so tired we can barely think straight.

Sleep is welcome respite and in my dreams I see you, Siân – as clear as anything! Are you working your magic, my love? Are you reaching out, comforting me through your talent, your gift? I strongly believe that you are; that our minds are meeting… It is what gets me through these long, difficult days. I see you in dreams. I talk to you – I hear your voice!

5th January 1916

Blwyddyn Newydd Dda! Nothing new to report in Laventie – the drudgery of trench life continues, although the weather has been kinder to us these past few days.

Siân – this might sound crazy, but sometimes I really do believe that you are here, beside me, in these cold, filthy trenches. I know that you are close; my dreams are lucid, vivid and I hear and see you all so clearly.

4th April 1916

I believe we will be moving soon, manning the front in Nord-Pas-de-Calais. We have certainly had our turn at the drudgery of the trenches. The months have been monotonous, with little change occurring and each day very much like the last.

I have become resigned to my time out here but I have to say that nothing we are made to do gives us any feeling of resentment. We know we have a job to do and we have become like brothers, fond of our country and each other.

When we are reunited, I shall look back on the rats, the trenches, the lice, the mud and the rain and bask in the fact that I am with you, Siân. Each night I lie on the floor of the trench and tell myself that I am strong, because I have gone one more day without you.

Chapter III

The sun cut through the windowpanes, assailing Caryl with its long, slanting arrows of light. She wore shades and was nursing a cup of black, bitter coffee.

"Not hungry?" Gene sliced open his croissant with a butter knife.

She shook her head, averting her gaze toward the breakfast bar. Last night's dream lingered, making her feel queasy and unwell. She'd dreamt something else, too; something about being cradled in the arms of trees, blood dripping from their stripped, flayed bark.

Gene was reading *The Daily Mail*, a newspaper she loathed. He'd grabbed a copy from the rack when they'd come down for breakfast earlier. It was yesterday's edition, but at least it was in English, at least it was familiar. It seemed to have made his morning.

"You all right?" He lifted his face and scowled. "I wish you'd take those glasses off."

"Wish you hadn't chosen to sit in the sun like this."

"We can move." He gestured with a listless flick of his hand. "There's a free table over there."

"It's fine." She frowned and firmed her jaw. "Got a headache."

He grunted, tutted, then said: "Don't think it's a good idea you trying this evening." She leaned back in her seat, arms tightly folded across her chest. "You need recovery time. A chance to heal, Caryl."

29

Anger flared within her. "The whole point of me being here…"

"I know, I know." His raised both hands in a placating gesture. "But it's dangerous, and I can see…"

"Don't want to talk about it."

Blood rose to his face, silencing him. He pushed his plate away, muttering to himself.

Had he failed to grasp the importance of this trip? She doubted he'd the imagination to understand the living hell people like Huw went through – men who sacrificed their freedom so that their children and grandchildren could enjoy theirs.

He pushed the last of his croissant into his mouth, then mumbled, "Going for a smoke. Coming?"

They stood outside in the garden beside the rhododendrons, a sudden breeze feeling like warm breath on her skin. "Sure I saw him," she said at last, her anger slipping away. "He was lying in a shell hole, dug right in. The dead scattered around him."

He pulled on his cigarette, eyes squinting into slits. "You don't have to rush this. We have the room for a week, and…"

"It's better on a full moon, remember? And the forecast's good."

They started walking alongside the hotel, following a gravelled path to the front of the building. Mametz's streets were quiet; there was hardly any traffic on the road. They passed the signs pointing the way to the Welsh memorial and Dantzig Alley British Cemetery. Gene flicked his cigarette to the ground, stopped and stomped it into the gravel.

Caryl was thirty-eight, and growing increasingly aware of her own mortality. These days, she felt fragile – desperately afraid of everything and anything, it seemed. She didn't know what she wanted; wasn't sure of anything anymore.

She knew that life wasn't long and that the window of opportunity was fleeting; precious. Sometimes, she could hear the sand falling in her own personal hourglass. Could feel the window shrinking, the darkness closing in…

She'd heard the phrase "You can never truly know a person" many times, but a desperate part of her wanted that to be untrue. She glanced at Gene, wondering what hopes and dreams he harboured. It was disturbing putting herself in his shoes, knowing what she knew about herself. Knowing how she felt about him; how she felt about Jake.

The way his face was twitching suggested that he was building up to something. Whatever it was, it had been there since their visit to her parents' house in March.

"I found Mametz Wood eerie," he said suddenly, snapping her from her thoughts.

She absently rubbed her hands together. "It's an eerie place," she agreed.

They perched on a bench beside a life-sized bronze statue of a soldier. Gene reached into his coat pocket, pulled out his Marlboros. Slotted a cigarette into his mouth and offered one to Caryl.

31

She shook her head, glancing at the soldier standing sternly over them.

"Shortly before we left," he said, "I did some research of my own. Found out how some of these hard-nosed army types admitted to seeing some pretty weird stuff in Mametz Wood."

She watched him light his cigarette, then suggested, "Perhaps they have a little of what I have."

"Visitors had the sensation of being watched – feeling dozens of eyes on them as they've explored the wood. There's been reports of bugle calls; the ghostly sounds of battle re-enactment...

"There's this one account," he sniffed, breathing smoke out of his nostrils, "where this guy saw a girl in Mametz Wood, lying there slumped against a tree, a sort of relieved smile on her face. Which doesn't make any sense, but anyway..." He gazed at the cigarette smouldering between his fingers. "The guy shouted and then she just vanished... as if into thin air." He grabbed his coat collar, pulled it close. "That one stood out, amongst the usual soldier and orb sightings." He shrugged. "Don't know why, but I read up on a lot of supernatural stuff before coming out here. Not usually a fan of ghost stories and such."

"I believe the past wants to be reawakened," she said quietly, urgently. "I feel it calling, Gene. In my subconscious; my dreams." Her gaze dropped, she stared into space. Then, shaking her head, looking up: "I felt connected to the wood...like I'd been there before, you know? And I felt a presence, pulling me, trying to drive me among the trees. It was so close, I could almost touch it. But I was afraid of it, too."

His eyes drifted over the shutters across the windows of the hotel opposite. "Maybe it's not something to be frightened of," he mused. "Perhaps it's… good. Harmonious, even." He chuckled, shrugged, drew on his cigarette. "Perhaps it didn't come from the past, whatever it was that came to you like that back there."

He got to his feet, flicked his cigarette to the floor. Ground it out with the heel of his shoe. She rubbed her arms, recalling that dream where the branches had grabbed her, holding her still, close and tight.

"I'd like to walk over to the cemetery this afternoon," she said. "Nan thought he might have been buried there, although his name isn't in the register. His name's etched on the Memorial to the Missing at Thiepval, though."

"The cemetery's just along here?" He gestured in the direction of the road.

"Yes. Just a short walk."

He nodded. That was sealed, then.

***

Excerpts from the diary of Pte Huw Price: -

4th June 1916

I saw my first dead body today. His name had been Hughes, shot to pieces at his post in the trench we dug yesterday. Found by Fritz while we were on

33

reconnaissance. His body was riddled with holes and with his innocent, almost serene expression, he looked little more than a boy who had laid down and fallen asleep with his eyes open. I got thinking then… At the end, had he been scared? Calm? Had he known what was about to happen? Did he have family? He died here alone without comfort or companionship. No one is born alone and no one should die alone.

The others dug his grave while I prepared the body. I found a photograph in his coat of a pretty girl with long dark hair. Could he have loved the girl as deeply as I love you, Siân? How cruel and sad that he should be denied a life with her.

I wrapped the body in oil skin, then we buried him, each taking turns to say a few words. As the first shovelfuls of dirt landed, the selfish thought of this could have been me could not be helped by my aching heart.

After we had finished, we feared another German assault, so we kept constant obs throughout the night, although orders to pursue the Germans in the morning filled me with both excitement and dread.

5th June 1916

I killed a man – what a truly sickening thing for me to have to write. If only you were here to talk to, Siân; I am scared of what I am becoming out here.

It happened this afternoon, on the outskirts of Festubert. We had been drifting to the west, having almost given up our pursuit of Fritz. Then we saw them – clad in grey tunics, coats and caps – running for the cover of the trees. There were five in total and they knew we were on to them.

It has been raining heavily so visibility was poor. Nonetheless, we aimed and let go, the German patrol dispersing under a hail of our bullets. I was thinking of Hughes as I went after one man, who was sprinting toward a chapel on the side of a road. I thought of the praise I would get if I shot him, although my excitement was tempered by the most awful fear imaginable.

The German reached the chapel and was just about to push through when he looked around – that was when I crouched, took aim and let go, dropping the man with a single shot from my rifle.

I felt elated, euphoric; Lewis reached my side, gripping my shoulder and shaking me, grinning: "Well done, well done."

The other chaps joined us, patting my cheek and commending me for my efforts. Then, straightening, ever-watchful, we made our way toward the chapel with the rain lashing down hard on us.

We reached the building and the man's motionless body. Dowie kicked the German, but he did not move, did not respond. We were satisfied that he was dead. Lewis pushed open the door and we all peered inside. There was nobody within, just a lot of dust and debris cluttering the floor. We focused our attentions on the soldier, turning him over and gazing into his face. His cap was off, his short blond hair spattered with mud and soil. I crouched and searched his coat. In one of the pockets I found a small bible, well-thumbed and torn at the edges.

Written on the fly-leaf in a child's handwriting was the single word Dada.

The men were quick to heap their praises and compliments on me, but the euphoria passed and was quickly replaced by a numbness and a sense of regret, over what I had done.

We held position for a couple of hours, waiting to see if the Germans would return. Then, at last, we gave up and marched on to Givenchy, cold, tired, and wet. All the while, I could not shake the dead soldier's face, or the bible with the child's handwriting in, out of my head. I kept thinking that somewhere in that soldier's fatherland was a little child who called him "Dada."

6th June 1916

Siân, how I wish I could talk to you – you realise how much you truly miss someone when something happens, good or bad, and the one person you want to tell is the person who is not there.

I had a nightmare last night. I was trying to find you, but it was so densely dark and foggy that I could not make you out at all. I remember feeling horribly disorientated as I called out your name, but I do not think you ever heard me.

This ties in with a feeling that I have had since leaving Laventie; a silly notion really, but it nags away all the same. I keep thinking that something bad is going to happen to me. I hope you do not think me paranoid, it is just the way I have been feeling. Hopefully, I will read back on this someday and laugh, although it is strange... It's like something bad has happened, but it just hasn't reached me yet. Whatever it is, it's coming... and I am just not ready for it. I mean, to let go. I am not making any sense here; I am weary and confused, weighed down by worry and fatigue all the time.

I try and visualise your face in the darkness, but all I see is Hughes' face, or the dead German's. Why do I not dream of you now? Just thinking about it fills me with such tremendous sadness.

The trench is quiet and the other chaps sound asleep. One of the sandbags has split and I hear soil pattering the ground – a slow, sibilant hiss. It keeps distracting my train of thought, setting my nerves on edge. It has awakened something inside that I cannot quite describe but frightens me, nonetheless.

Chapter IV

They pushed through the gate and entered Dantzig Alley British Cemetery. At the end of the grounds rose a cross, THEIR NAME LIVETH FOR EVERMORE chiselled on its base. Flowers and wreaths lay scattered around it.

Caryl picked up the Cemetery Register, vainly searching its pages for Huw. As Nan'd said, his name wasn't there, despite this being the most likely place for him to have been buried.

Caryl raised her sunglasses, swiftly rubbed her eyes. The sudden surge of emotion made her want to tell Gene everything, freeing herself of guilt. She sniffed, pushed her glasses up. No. If there was a time, it wasn't now.

Jake knew about Gene, Gene didn't know about Jake. Jake had been in and out of her life since she was nineteen; they'd got together shortly after college and were together five years. She'd been with Gene for eighteen months now and he was the only boyfriend she'd ever introduced her parents to. He was practical, pragmatic and conservative; she knew right away that they'd approve.

But, after introducing him to her parents, their inevitable approval had troubled and disturbed her. For days afterwards, she'd seriously considered breaking up with him, just to spite her father and mother.

Her issues with her parents were complex, their approval of Gene rousing a rebellious streak that had long been dormant.

"Caryl?" Gene placed a hand on her arm, shaking it, causing her to start and blink out of her thoughts. She glanced at the information board he'd been studying. "This is now the final resting place of over 2,000 servicemen," he read aloud, "of whom some 500 remain unidentified."

Her eyes ghosted over the unnamed graves beside them, the simple words A SOLDIER OF THE GREAT WAR chiselled on the headstones.

"I'll find you," Caryl breathed. "I'll show you how you endured."

They turned and wandered the grounds, trees rustling around them. Gene tugged her sleeve, flashed her an uneasy smile. "Shall we go?"

Caryl's head was filled with Nan and Huw as they followed the road back to Mametz. There was barely any light in the sky, despite the time of year. Great grey swathes of cloud gathered ominously, threatening rain.

They didn't go straight to the hotel, choosing to visit a café instead. It was small and quiet, only a few people inside at round rickety tables and in the armchairs. They chose a table in the corner, near the bar. The wallpaper was patterned with what looked like entwining branches, snaking and swirling around each other into insane designs. Twisting, circling, they swallowed themselves like the Ouroboros. Caryl took off her sunglasses, laid them on the table. Massaged her brow with her fingers in slow, circular motions.

As Gene ordered coffees, she visualised her visit to Nan's house in March. Nan's furniture had still been there; hadn't been moved or packed up yet. She had chosen a spot on the carpet, sat down and spread Nan's belongings out in front of her – photographs; a doll that Nan had owned since childhood; Nan's satin wedding gown and veil; diaries Nan'd kept that documented her scrying. From the diaries, Caryl had gleaned how supportive Huw had been, helping Siân cope with the nightmares and hallucinations she'd endured. He'd been her rock, her constant. When he'd died, Nan'd lost everything.

Caryl hadn't needed much as there'd been plenty of Nan around – skin flakes sifting through the air or gathered upon surfaces throughout the room. She'd uttered the arcane words, spells; used the moon through the window to create the bridge, the tunnel, back to another day, another time completely.

The sudden sight of Nan had been shocking – curled up like a question mark in her chair, her arms folded, fingers gripping scrawny shoulders, wrinkled, yellow flesh wrapping brittle bones like clingfilm.

"Nan…" Caryl had said her name, over and over, trying to get an acknowledgment, a reaction. "Nan, I'm here. It's me, Caryl."

Siân's eyes had cleared of fog – and Caryl had taken the chance, saying all that she'd needed to say, hoping to provide comfort, hope, and reassurance in Nan's last moments.

Gene sat down, breaking her reverie. "Ordered us Cappuccinos."

She picked up her glasses, pushed them back on her face. Drew back the sleeve of her jacket and stroked the scars on her arm.

"You know what Mum said about Nan," she frowned, "after Nan'd died?"

Gene contemplated this for a moment. "No," he said at last.

"She said it was the lunacy that got her. That it broke her mind, like everybody knew it would." She paused to allow silence, then added: "Said this in front of me. Despite knowing that I have this…thing; this so-called 'gift'." A deep scowl momentarily contorted her features. "Mum was fortunate, see. It skipped a generation, missing her out completely."

"Caryl." He drummed his fingers on the tabletop. "They worry about you, that's all."

She twisted her face away. "I'm a problem that they can't fix. They're exasperated by me."

The waiter placed their coffees down along with the bill, then turned and headed for the bar again.

"Is that how you see yourself?" Gene gingerly softened his voice. "A problem that needs fixing?"

"Why do you feel the need to defend them all the time?"

He heaved an exaggerated sigh. "I think they worry about you, that's all. They feel like there's a barrier up, which they can't break through."

She shook her head, muttered under her breath.

"I chatted with your Mum when we saw them last."

"Talking about me behind my back, were you?"

"It wasn't like that." He leaned back in his seat, frowning. "It made me realise that bridges need to be built. I mean, she cares about you; very much so. Your father, too. They think it's great that you were close to Siân. That you're so locked in your family's history. Sara never had much of a relationship with Siân, who never stopped grieving after your grandfather died." He shuffled forward, the chair legs squeaking. "Your mother felt the impact of that, I think. Having to live in the shadow of her grief. And don't forget, Sara was denied a father – that must have been hard, growing up without knowing him. But your mother was never jealous of your relationship with Siân. In fact, she was grateful." He allowed for a moment's pause before adding: "It was obvious that you were struggling."

Her fingers slipped away from her scars.

She recalled sitting in the kitchen of her parents' house in February, going through some of Nan's personal artefacts in cardboard boxes. They'd come across Siân's wedding ring; the one Huw had chosen for her, with its diamond and two sapphires.

"You can't take that," Mum'd said quickly, exchanging a glance with Gene; a peculiar look that had unsettled Caryl greatly.

Jake surfaced in her mind again. She wanted him, that's what this was about, really. But Jake had let her down, time and time again. She didn't think he could change. Perhaps it was time to let go; to forget him and move on at last.

They finished their coffees, settled the bill with the waiter. Left the café and crossed the road toward the waiting hotel. The dark clouds had shifted and the sky was blue, the sun warm and bright. They sat beside each other on rusted chairs, in the patioed area outside the conservatory. Gene lit another of his cigarettes, Caryl feeling his need to speak pressing behind the silence.

"What was it like growing up with your Mum and Dad?" he asked at last. "I mean, what was their relationship like?"

"They were a lot older than other parents," she shrugged. "My friends' parents. They seemed older, too. In their ways; their mannerisms. In their attitudes and values. It was…cloying growing up around them, I suppose." Caryl chewed her lower lip. "I think I can probably count the number of times I've seen them kiss, or hold hands, or show any kind of affection to the other, on the fingers of one hand." She held a hand up and wriggled her fingers at him.

"I think they love each other. They're just set in their ways, that's all. It's how they function."

"It's a tired, worn-out love." A humourless laugh twisted in her throat. "I've never wanted what they've got. It's like them being together, they've lost something – a spark; an integral part of themselves." She tilted her face to the sun. "Anyway, I don't know how they are, despite growing up around them. I think a lot has been concealed from me, I really do."

43

"You think they're unhappy?"

"I think they have an idea of love, but they've never really experienced it. Don't think they ever got there."

A gust of wind caused the willows in the gardens to shake, to sigh. It reminded her of that dream with the trees.

"I think of Huw and Siân a lot," she whispered. "What they had was special, you know?" She threw him a tentative glance. "Do you think a love like that can be...difficult for others? I mean, can it be too much to live up to? To hope for; to wish for themselves?"

"Huw was taken from Siân so young..."

"But at least they got to experience it, even if it was fleeting. No one can take that away from them."

She unconsciously rubbed her scars again.

"Why do you hurt yourself?" he asked.

She stiffened slightly. "I'm never at peace." She swiftly pulled down her sleeves, feeling uncomfortable, exposed. "There's a war waging inside me. But at least out here there's purpose; a reason to be."

She clasped her hands together, expelled a ragged sigh. "When I was younger," she said, "I thought I could cut and see the thing inside. See it all shine out, radiant and true. But there was only ever pain... Albeit a different pain to what I was used to. It became something to focus on, helping me to forget all about the fear I was feeling."

She was about to mention Jake and how he liked to cut himself, too. How sometimes they did it together – our little battle scars, he'd call them. The ritual brought them close, although it pushed the rest of the world far, far away.

Gene stared into her face, his eyes steel-grey and distant. "I often wonder what I can do to see you smile." His brow furrowed. "You smile in my dreams, Caryl."

She leaned toward him, digging him playfully in the ribs. "You think you can save me, right? Is that what this is about?"

He gripped his knees, shook his head. "Don't make me into something I'm not." Then, after thinking it through: "I'm just trying to help. I do love you, you know."

"My knight in shining armour." She sucked in a deep breath, puffed out her cheeks, then exhaled. "My anxiety's through the roof. My flight or fight kicks in over the stupidest of fucking things."

He reached into his coat pocket, the muscles in his face twitching. Again, it felt like he was building up to something. Then the muscles relaxed, his fingers withdrew, the hand unclenched and empty.

Her headache was clearing, she was beginning to feel better. They retired to the hotel and grabbed a snack in the restaurant before the evening rush. Then, lounging on a sofa in the conservatory, they watched the sun go down behind the gardens.

"Remember," Gene said. "If you're not up for…"

"I'm fine, really."

They went to their room to pack Siân's things in Caryl's rucksack. Caryl drifted to the window, gazed out at the bright full moon.

Her skin tingled, the small hairs on her arms stood on end.

She could harvest so much tonight.

***

Excerpts from the diary of Pte Huw Price: -

9th June 1916

I think we will be moving soon, to the neighbourhood of St. Pol, for further training.

I am no longer so frightened. Just numb, I suppose; taking each day as it comes. Not looking back. Not looking forward, either. I am still having anxiety attacks, which wake me up at night and leave me sleep deprived and low.

I am sure we will be together soon, Siân. When we are reunited, I shall look back on this with such relief. That I am me; not this wreck of a so-called soldier.

28th June 1916

Sorry for the lengthy silence, my love, but I have had little writing time and am weary and footsore from marching. We are digging trenches again and making practice attacks, preparing ourselves for battle. We are moving further south to the Somme valley in the next day or so, to join II Corps. Fear is everywhere – in the eyes of the boys and in the faces of our enemy, too. I feel it most in quiet, reflective moments, when I am tired and alone with far too much time on my hands.

5th July 1916

Another quick note as things are speeding up, moving to an end... We have received our orders for attacking the German Second Line along the Bazentin Ridge to the north of Mametz Wood. My heart is banging like a drum! The wood is flanked on both sides by trenches that are held by the enemy, elements of the German Lehr Infantry Regiment and 163rd Infantry Regiment.

Siân – I wish my dreams were as lucid and vivid as they were when I first arrived. What I would give to see or hear you again, even in dream.

6th July 1916

Brigadier-General Evans and Lieutenant Colonel ap Rhys Pryce are conducting a reconnaissance this morning of the ground over which the 115th Brigade will advance. We have already been told that Mametz Wood is "very dense, with thick undergrowth" and "movement for infantry not easy" – not helped by the heavy shelling, which has uprooted trees and made advancement trickier. Bullets and shrapnel burst overhead with frightening regularity and a shell claimed two NCOs in the early hours of this morning. I try not to think about it, immersing myself in whatever work I can find.

I look into the eyes of the other men and see my own fear and aloneness reflected at me. It is this inescapable feeling of abandonment and loneliness amid a crowd that is, for me, the essence of the dark night of the soul.

I dreamed last night for the first time in a while. We were camped close to Mametz Wood, preparing for battle. Hughes was beside me, and as we got talking he suddenly became the German soldier that I had killed near Festubert. I felt a surge of emotion and wanted to offload to him how sorry I was, that I had not stopped thinking about him since it happened, when this enormous shadow descended...

Something was moving through the wood at terrific speed. I cannot explain it; it was like the past, present and future converging to form an absence, a void. Trees splintered and snapped, branches spinning off in all directions as soldiers screamed and scrabbled for purchase, clinging to rocks and trees for dear life.

I grabbed hold of a rock but felt myself shake and slide inexorably toward it. I knew it would take us all; suddenly, it felt easier to let go. To surrender myself and let it have its way with me. That was when this dreadful sense of hopelessness descended and as I looked around I saw that I was alone. All the soldiers had gone. Then the void rushed forward and consumed me utterly, and I gasped awake, my heart hammering, my body coated in cold clammy sweat.

Chapter V

Under the silvery moon, over a shadow-strewn field, Caryl marched with determination etched across her face. Gene was barely managing to keep up behind.

She walked with conviction, with purpose, charged with energy and intent, ready to turn back the days, the years, decades. She'd never felt so powerful. Past, present and future would converge – she'd tear down walls of space and time to find him.

Two hundred yards from the wood, she shrugged off her bag and opened it, putting the contents on the ground. She set the last item down, threw her head back and stared at the bright full moon. Light filled her eyes, her head, her thoughts. She was no longer aware of Gene; only the energy flowing through her body, her veins. "You are universal and constant," she sighed. "In the dark of night, You shine down upon me and bathe me in Your light and love."

Everything was folding, spinning and changing. New shapes formed as the present rapidly crumbled. Gene was cut adrift, lost to her. Cryptic words spilled from her mouth, drawing down the moon and reawakening battle…

Cordite and gas invaded her nostrils; so too the stench of stagnant water, decayed sandbags and rot. The earth was littered with bodies, some bandaged, some splintered, some motionless. Caryl saw blurred movement – soldiers – darting, leaping and dodging through the thick smog ahead. A shell exploded; the dull chatter of machine gun fire could be heard. She found her feet and ran, knowing time was against her, the opportunity shrinking fast.

The blasted stumps of trees smouldered, flames licking about them. Ahead, a mound of writhing figures was burrowing into the ground to shelter from gunfire. Bullets flew but didn't land; she wasn't solid, wasn't quite corporeal. Glancing down, she noticed a boy – must have been in his teens – by her feet, eyes open, lips trembling, the top of his head completely missing. She watched in horror as his eyes clouded; then, moments later, he was gone – whisked away from the filth, mud and shit of the battlefield.

She resumed her search, her heart thumping like a wild animal trying to escape her chest. She noticed amongst a tide of bodies a figure in a shell-hole, breathing hard and fast, spread out on the ground with his hands clasped around his middle. It was almost as though he was trying to say something, but all that escaped his lips were little grunts, gasps and sighs.

She approached hesitantly, bullets whistling, shrieking around her. Then, refocusing her gaze, concentrating, she recognised him – the same face as the one in Nan's photographs; the very person she'd been searching for…

Something warm and bright blossomed inside her.

He looked up, his features splattered with mud and gore. His tunic was torn, ripped and drenched in blood.

See me, she willed. Look. Notice. See me!

Their gazes locked, his eyes widened; then, trying to sit up, a strange expression rippled his face: one of surprise, bewilderment and – yes! – recognition…

In that moment, she knew he could see her, he knew she was there.

She crawled into the shell-hole with him, taking one of his hands, squeezing it hard. She was solid now. Real. Beneath the sliminess of the mud, she felt his callused fingers close.

Another shell thudded close by. Caryl didn't blink.

"Siân? Siân…that really you?" A cracked sob escaped him. "I knew you'd come. But…how?" He laughed weakly, coughing blood.

Caryl wiped tears from her cheeks. "No," she said, shaking her head, "not Siân. Caryl. Your granddaughter."

His fingers were tight – vice-like – around hers, like he never wanted to let go. She couldn't believe she was holding him like this.

The bodies of soldiers flickered around her, skipping and sinking like loose television images.

"I wanted to come and sit with you," she explained. "Didn't want you to be alone. Siân didn't; she tried to find you, see. She…she wanted to be here. She did all she could, then I took it upon myself to finish her work."

His smile silenced her – a bright, wide, genuine smile. It carried none of the melancholy from the photographs.

"You're beautiful," he whispered.

His fingers pressed and twisted around hers, then she cradled and nestled his head in the crook of her arm.

Something hit her then, hard, in the chest and everything spun and wheeled in sickeningly breakneck fashion. She involuntarily let go his hand as he let out one last gasp. The screaming, shouting and machine gun chatter shrank away – suddenly, deathly silence reigned.

Her own ragged breathing punctuated the silence. Panic engulfed her, her entire body felt like it was on fire.

She clasped a hand to her chest, brought it away again. Saw her whole palm was slick with black blood.

Gene kneeled, his eyes large, wild, white. He was with her again, she was back where she was supposed to be and, as he tried to put his arms around her, she screamed; he let go quickly, hands clawing and flexing at his sides.

Something chimed on the ground beside her, catching the light of the moon. A gold ring studded with a diamond and two sapphires. Must have come from his pocket, although he hadn't noticed, hadn't seen it fall.

A grimace twisted his lips. "God, Caryl, what…?"

She spat blood. "Think I got shot."

"I-I'll get help," he gasped, looking around at the night; the fields; Mametz Wood.

As he went to stand, she snatched out, seizing his arm. "I saw him. And in his last moments, I made it bearable, Gene."

52

She let go.

He stood swiftly, gasping "Back as soon as I can. Promise."

She blinked and turned and gazed at the ring, finally realising what had been on his mind all this time.

***

Excerpt from the diary of Pte Huw Price: -

7th July 1916

Despite it being so dismally cold, grey and wet, the chaps are in fine voice, singing their hearts out to 'Jesus, Lover Of My Soul' to the tune of 'Aberystwyth'. Not even a particularly violent hailstorm could diminish their words.

Lt. Colonel Carden has done his rounds, assuring us that we will take the wood. A smoke screen will conceal our approach, which has alleviated fears a little.

I need to stay calm, need to be an example. There are young boys here, and the fear in their eyes is heart-breaking to behold. Most have never fired a round in combat, and have only used broomsticks, rather than rifles, at drill practice.

We go over in two hours' time. Siân, if the worst does happen, I know that I live on – in you, in Sara. I know that I will endure! Life is precious – we must make the most of every second. Each cherished moment must count!

Do you remember the sandbag I mentioned in a previous entry? Well, when the shells aren't bursting, or the machine guns roaring, I hear it – the sand falling, pattering – like time whispering ever-so-softly away. It fills me with urgency, clouding my heart and thoughts with fear.

I cannot stop thinking about that soldier I killed. If I could turn back time, I would, without a moment's hesitation, put myself in a position where I would not have had to kill that man. I think I die a little every time I think of him. We are the same when it comes down to it, even the men waiting for us now, under the cover of the trees, at the base of this slope. I do not want to kill a single one of them, either.

Siân – if I did come back, what will you think of me? Will you still love me, knowing that I am a killer? That I have deprived a child of his father? I do not know if I deserve to return home and live a life of comfort anyway.

I do not know what I am trying to say here, everything is so sad and wrong, all at the same time. If anything does happen, do not mourn long – live your lives to the full, full in the fullest of God. I want you both to be happy, to know and feel joy again!

Love is the blessed of gifts, and I have been loved. No one can take that away from me. I must make an island for myself and hold onto that love.

Thoughts are whizzing around inside my brain and I can barely rein them in. The truth is, I am most dreadfully scared. I can scarcely hold my pen my hand is shaking so. All sorts of nonsense springs

54

from my mind and the fear is compounded by the fact that you never feature in my dreams anymore. I fear that I have lost you, that I am completely cut adrift.

And that feeling of doom … well, it never goes away. It seems to strengthen with each passing minute, with every passing second.

I do not want to die out here alone. I am filled with dread by whatever it is that is coming… and it's coming.

It is so close, I can almost touch it.

55

Chapter VI

Caryl snatched up the ring, then turned and crawled on all fours into the enveloping darkness of the wood. Each time she breathed, pain flared in her ribs, causing her to gasp, to cry out, scream. Branches clawed at her, tearing, snagging her jacket, raking the scarred flesh beneath.

She cast off her rucksack, the contents spilling out across the ground. She rolled onto her back, gazing up at the sky. The moon was a pale, scratched disc behind a tangle of gnarled branches and ivy. She squeezed the ring into her pocket, then closed her eyes and whimpered through clenched teeth, tears flowing down her mud-stained cheeks.

She tried controlling her breathing, but the pain was intense enough to cause her to scream again, her voice sounding unnatural and animalistic in her own ears.

She sat up and shuffled back, twigs and leaves crunching beneath her. She reached a tree and reclined against it, staring through the foliage at the pitch-dark field beyond.

Her vision shimmered, dimmed. Gradually, her thoughts turned inward…

She was a child again, talking to her Nan in Nan's front room. Caryl had her whole life ahead of her and things would be different, she vowed – things would be better this time. She'd seen how it could go wrong and she promised she wouldn't make the same mistakes.

Was she scrying?

Was this a warning from the future?

Nan placed a hand on top of her head, fingers gently caressing her hair.

I discern loops and terrible dark patterns…

Caryl's eyes snapped open.

She gasped loudly, deeply, the pain immense, pulsing through her like fire. Nan was gone and she was here, in the wood, where she'd been all along.

She'd no concept of time – minutes, hours, perhaps even decades might have passed. Shrubs and branches had reopened the scars across her arms; peering down, she saw the leaf-strewn ground black and slick with her blood. It felt as though she'd given herself to this place, a sacrifice for him – the soul she'd come here to comfort. And she'd succeeded, too; she'd found him, completing Nan's work, linking them together again. It was something to hold onto now.

A black wave crashed over her, then voices brought her back to herself, lights dancing, flashing, weaving ahead. French men were conversing in the field, then another voice – a familiar voice – started calling to her.

She tried standing, but the pain was too much, making her shrink, wither and fold. She didn't want to get up anyway; felt so safe in the twisted arms of the trees. They enveloped her like in that dream, pulling her close, holding her tight. Pressing against her trembling flesh like the edges of razorblades. Turning, reaching, she scratched at the bark with her fingernails. Watched blood erupt, trickling down the trunk toward the roots.

Gene kept calling, over and over. Caryl couldn't respond, couldn't reply. That black wave was returning, promising to wipe her out and take her away for good. Like Gene had said, perhaps it wasn't anything to be frightened of.

Twigs snapped and bushes rustled. The gruff voices grew louder, and more urgent. Caryl shuddered as a group of shadowy figures clustered near. It was getting cold, so very cold. Darkness was beginning to swallow everything.

As a flashlight beam found her face, she breathed out her last and smiled.

The Sea And The Statues

Harriet sat in the corner in her favourite chair.

"Sing to me, Danielle; sing to me," she said. Danielle put Drummy to bed. The clock on the wall chimed seven.

"Mummy, Drummy can't get to sleep."

"Drummy *will* sleep. Come over and sing to me." Danielle sighed and stamped her little foot before falling to Harriet's feet. She took hold of her mother's hand.

"What shall I sing to you, Mummy?"

Harriet could see Danielle, but it was different to what Danielle looked like. In her mind she had perfect round blue eyes and beautiful blond hair. "Anything you like."

So Danielle sang her favourite song and both voice and sea merged into one harmonious sound. Harriet felt the tears slide down her cheeks.

When Danielle had finished, she let go of her mother's hand and gazed up at her room. "I wonder if Drummy can dream. Like I can."

"Isn't he asleep yet?"

"No. He's sitting in bed listening to the sea. Mummy, do dreams come true?"

"Sometimes. What is it you dream, Danielle?"

The girl paused, then paced the room. She kept glaring up at the clock. Finally she spoke. "I dream Drummy is alive. That he can talk back to me and we can play hopscotch on the beach. Mummy, do you think there are other people out there?"

59

"Of course there are. Someday I'm sure you'll meet somebody. What's the time?"

"Somebody *not* a statue?"

"Is it gone seven?" Harriet didn't think about the statues too much. She had grown to accept them.

"Not yet."

"I don't believe you, young lady. Come on, let's get you to bed. Drummy needs the company."

***

The morning was golden and clear. Slants of sunshine cut through the crystal panes and cast Drummy in a warm glow. The puppet sat lifeless on the cabinet, smiling at no-one in particular.

Danielle was sitting at the table stirring her cereal in the milk, staring at Drummy. She winked at him and spooned herself some food.

***

And the day grew like any other day and Danielle took her mother out across the beach. She pushed Harriet along in her wheelchair. Harriet sat, quite content, enjoying the sun's warmth on her skin and the sound of the lazy waves. She smiled.

"Is the sun bright this morning?"

Danielle looked up. "Yes, Mummy. There isn't a single cloud in the sky!"

"Oh dear. Then you can't play your favourite game today."

"Oh wait! I *can* see one. It looks like… it looks like our house by the sea. I can see the slanting roof and if I look hard, the wind-chimes through my bedroom window."

"Once, when Mummy had her sight and you hadn't even been born, I used to lie in the fields and make pictures with the clouds…"

"Maybe you'll see again one day."

Harriet turned her head. It was the only part of her body she could move. "You're changing direction."

"I had to, Mummy. There was a statue in the way."

"A pretty statue?"

"A young boy. He's got ever such a pretty face and long locks of hair. I wonder if he ever lived. Do you think that's what happens to your body, Mummy, when you go to heaven? Does it turn into a statue?"

Harriet just laughed.

***

Just of late, the statues had been building up. New ones were appearing all the time. Each one always caught a glimpse of Danielle before Danielle caught a glimpse of them.

The wind picked up and the lazy waves began to roar. Danielle put a blanket around her mother. "Shall we go now, Mummy?"

"Yes, dear. The wind is cold and the sea is restless."

"Good. I'm missing Drummy."

A bout of melancholia momentarily hung over Harriet. It was triggered by her usual twinges of

61

guilt. Perhaps Harriet should not have brought up the child by the sea; perhaps she could have been mingled with others. No. It would have been hard.

Danielle giggled. "That new cloud looks like a snake with its tongue poking out."

"You and your strange imagination. Come on, let's hurry. There might be a storm. How quickly the weather changes."

The child steered her mother around statues and saw the house was in sight.

Then she stopped.

There was a long pause. The wind howled, cold on Harriet's face. "What's wrong? Why have we stopped?"

"*Hush,* Mummy! In the distance I can see someone…I can see him walking about!"

"What does he look like?"

"*Shush!* He's coming closer. Oh Mummy, what shall I do?" The wind blew harder and Harriet shivered.

The stranger walked closer and he lifted his head. Danielle smiled at him. For Harriet, the period of waiting was agonizing.

Then – "*Danielle!* Who is he?"

"Oh Mummy, I was wrong. It was just another statue." Her disappointment sounded close to despair. Slowly they started moving again. They made their way back to the house in total silence.

***

That afternoon Danielle played with Drummy until she got bored. Then she prepared supper, careful not to cut herself whilst chopping the vegetables, and they ate in front of the fire. When the clock chimed seven, Danielle tucked Drummy into bed and helped Harriet from her chair on to the settee. She kissed her goodnight.

"Don't forget to call if you need anything," she said.

"I won't, angel," replied Harriet.

Danielle ascended the wooden steps and lay on her bed. The window was open and the wind whistled in and stroked the wind-chimes.

She was feeling better.

"Goodnight Drummy," she said, and kissed her doll. Then she rolled over and played with the snakes in her hair until she fell asleep.

Night In Our Veins

"What are you doing?"

Ethan looked up, and I managed to catch a glimpse of the picture he was drawing in his sketchbook – some demonic-looking creature with scabrous wings and the blackest of eyes.

"It's what's been calling me," he said. "The only thing that makes sense."

"What is it?"

"Don't know," he replied, shrugging. "But it wants me. And the emptier and more lost I am the better." He turned back to his work, picking up a piece of charcoal from off the table.

I left him to his art, feeling uneasy and concerned.

Ethan and I ventured out that night for the first time in a long time, finding a quiet corner in an otherwise bustling *The Raven Inn*. I thought going to the pub might do us both some good, but he was as distant and morose as ever.

I tried engaging him in conversation. "I rang my brother up earlier."

He sneered but said nothing.

"He thinks I should contact my parents. Maybe they've changed. What do you think?"

He put his bottle of Diamond White down on the table, then wagged his finger at me. "Your parents are selfish, self-satisfied people. They want you to embrace everything they value." He reached out, touching me lightly on the arm. "You should have grown up like them, didn't you know? Career-minded. Conservative. Deathly dull and completely uninspiring."

"Alex says they want to mend things. They want to know me again."

He shot to his feet, knocking into the table, clearly exasperated. "I'm getting another bottle. Do you want one?"

I shook my head and he wheeled away, jostling his way to the bar.

Later, as we stepped out into the night, I told him, "Sorry."

Ethan's shoulders sagged and he looked heavenwards.

"It's just that… I've been thinking a lot about my family lately, you know?"

"Why?" he said. "After what they put you through, you should just fucking forget them. Forget they ever existed."

"It's not as easy as that…"

"They don't mean anything to you anymore, right? You've moved on. What's the point in looking back?"

I stared down at the pavement, thinking: *Why can I never find the right words in an emotional conflict?*

"Hey," he said, softening his voice, touching my shoulder. "I want to take you somewhere."

He led me to a church on the outskirts of Cosham. It was run-down and boarded up, its walls smeared with graffiti. The silence and stillness of the place felt dislocating, and I shivered beneath my jacket. "Why are we here?"

Ethan didn't reply. He reached into his coat pocket and pulled out a bottle of Diamond White.

"Smuggled this out of the pub," he grinned, peering around me at the church. "By the way, you heard the legend about this place?"

I shook my head.

"Something moved in there and made itself at home. Hiding inside the church or in the graveyard somewhere, I'm not sure which." For some reason I thought of that strange creature he'd drawn in his sketchbook the other day.

He turned his gaze on me, his smile gone. "If you can prove you're serious, if you can show *it* what it wants, then it'll gladly take you in."

He necked his cider, then squeezed and cracked the bottle in his fist. Broken glass fell, sprinkling the earth. He held his hand up, inspecting the wound. "Don't bleed anymore," he whispered. "It's like the night's running through my veins."

"Come on," I said, taking hold of his arm. "Let's get out of here."

***

I woke the next morning to find Ethan gone; I was all alone in his bed. I forced myself up, shuffling out of the room and into the hall. His boots and coat were missing and a glance at the clock revealed I was due at work in under an hour. I dressed and was soon driving my rust-eaten Metro through town. I stayed away from the main road, choosing to pass the church we visited last night instead. It was there that I saw him, traipsing through the graveyard on his own.

You heard the legend about this place?

I stamped on the brake, pulling up on the outskirts of a housing estate. It didn't take long to find a payphone – there was one outside of a convenience store near the King Richard School. I told my boss I was suffering from a migraine, but I don't think he believed me. *Fuck him,* I thought, slamming down the phone.

To the west there was a hill overlooking the church. I walked to the top of it, watching Ethan use his shoulder to break through the church's double doors below.

I closed my eyes, listening to the branches of the trees clack around me. My mind backtracked; I reminisced over the first couple of months of our relationship, and how I'd thought – *I've never known anyone quite like Ethan.*

He was unique, beautiful, scary. He always wore black T-shirts, a long leather coat and a pair of scuffed Dr. Martens. To look at, he reminded me of that actor Vincent Gallo, from the movie *Buffalo '66*; pale, gaunt face, unkempt hair, intense blue eyes embedded in cavernous sockets. He said from the outset that he didn't believe in love, that he'd never had that feeling for anyone and probably never will. That wounded me at first, and perhaps a stupid part of me hoped to turn him around. Now I know better.

67

He let me move into his flat shortly after the fall out with my parents. Occasionally we'd go out drinking, but mostly we stayed in, ensconced within the flat's walls. Ethan would sit on the windowsill, staring through the glass with such intensity that I'd swear he was projecting images from his mind onto the dismal wastelands below.

He introduced me to poetry, reading aloud from the works of Plath, Poe and Larkin. We'd stay up into the early hours, reciting our favourite poems or listening to indie-rock on his beaten stereo. Sometimes Ethan would draw with charcoal, producing weird and disturbing images in his sketchbook. I think his winged demon disturbed me most, though. In time Ethan grew disinterested in art; he withdrew into himself – away from the world, and from me, too.

I remember the first time he caught me alone with my straight razor.

"We really do belong together," he said, an enigmatic smile flickering across his face.

I opened my eyes, blinking, refocusing on the world around me.

Ethan had finished his exploration of the church and was now pulling closed the gates. I thought about going down there and joining him, but I didn't really feel like it; I felt strangely hollow and detached from things.

I returned to my car and waited until he was out of sight, then drove up to Portsdown Hill. I parked in a secluded spot overlooking a grey sprawl of tired-looking tower blocks and houses. The sea on the horizon was clean and white, like a thin strip of mercury.

I opened the glove compartment and took out the plastic case inside. It might have been a snap-case for a pen, toothbrush or comb. I unclipped it and tipped out my straight razor.

I tilted the seat back and rolled up the sleeve of my shirt. I put the razor to my flesh and began cutting, Ethan's voice echoing around inside my head: *"If you can prove you're serious, if you can show* it *what it wants, then it'll gladly take you in..."*

I gasped, the blade slipping through my fingers, clattering onto the pedals by my feet. I lifted my arm up, staring in disbelief at what I discerned beneath the flesh...

***

The flat was silent, chilled. I threw my jacket onto the sofa and stood staring out of the window. The sky was grey and lightless and I prayed for rain to come and break the monotony. It reminded me that I hadn't cried in such a long time. Suddenly I heard a noise coming from the bathroom. I turned around, calling: "Ethan?"

I found him in the bathtub, his eyes fixed on nothing in particular on the wall. For a horrible moment I feared the worst. Then he blinked, the grin spreading across his face looking like the rictus of something long dead. "Found it," he breathed.

I turned away, prompting him to sit up in the bath and ask: "When you're ready, you'll come, right?"

"Yes," I said with my back to him. "You know I will."

I heard his razor scrape across the rim of the bathtub. I looked over my shoulder, watching him cut himself.

"I'm ready," he whispered. "Just waiting on you now. I never wanted to do this alone, remember?"

It's a comfort to the damned to have companions in misery, I thought, and wondered where I'd heard that from. A line from one of the poems we used to read, I supposed.

Something surfaced in his eyes then; something almost human, I sensed. He suppressed it, blinked it away.

"Cut me," I said.

He sneered as I offered him my arm. Then he stood up and slashed me.

Seconds later the razor dropped into the tub with a splash. "You too," he said, so faintly I wasn't sure I'd really heard the words.

He cupped his long, cold hands around my face and kissed me hard on the mouth, but I tasted absolutely nothing of him at all.

***

I followed him through the streets, past lines of shuttered shops and crooked townhouses. The moon looked like a rip in a sheet of black fabric. *Just another hole,* I thought, absently.

We reached our destination, clambered over the padlocked gates and dropped down into the grounds. Bone-white headstones and marble angels hovered in the darkness around us.

Ethan took hold of my elbow, guiding me toward the church doors. The pale moonlight fell in a spectral slat over that splintered entryway. Ethan pushed on through, produced a small torch from his pocket and flicked it on. Everything seemed buried beneath layers of dust and cobweb. His light paused momentarily at a wooden pew that had been pushed aside, and I saw the raised lid of a trapdoor.

We shuffled forward, Ethan crouching and pointing the beam down into the blackness. "There's a ladder set in the wall," he said. "Watch yourself." He carefully mounted the rungs. "Coming?"

I turned my body around and lowered my boot onto the first rung, then slowly followed him down. I reached the bottom, brushed the dust off my jeans and turned. He used the beam to show me that we were in a chamber as small and sparse as a tomb.

I gasped when I saw the statue; it looked so lifelike, so *real*.

Ethan's face twitched; a spasm that wasn't quite a smile. He put the torch in my hand so I could point the beam at it myself.

It looked like it was carved from onyx, its arms folded, its long-fingered hands gripping its bony shoulders. Scabrous wings protruded from its body.

71

It stood on a cracked plinth and, as I raised the beam, I swear I saw it smile.

I placed my hand to my chest, to my pounding heart, then took it away again. Thoughts of my family passed through my mind.

They want to mend things. Want to know me again.

I glanced nervously at Ethan. "What is it?"

"We have to show it." He stared at me, emotionless. "That we've passed the initiation. That we're ready and willing to submit."

He produced his straight razor from his pocket. Rolled up a sleeve and rested the blade against his arm. He pressed down, the flesh opening blackly.

I don't bleed anymore.

I glanced around again at the statue.

Its smile was clearer now, wider. Directed right at us.

I was shaking all over. *Mustn't let on I'm afraid*, I thought.

"Your go."

Ethan raised the gleaming blade in his hand and I rolled up the sleeve of my shirt. He cut me quickly, keenly, causing me to shut my eyes and close down and focus on detaching myself. I opened my eyes at last. The wound was deep. Blood was trickling down the inside of my arm.

I sensed movement and jerked the beam, seeing the statue step down from off its plinth. I tried to scream but no sound would come out. It shuffled forward, hooves clopping, wings unfurling, cupping its clawed hands around Ethan's face. Then I wheeled, bolting through darkness, groping for the rungs of the ladder and scrambling up them.

Near to the top I paused, twisted around and directed the beam into that sepulchral vault. I screamed at last for I could see the thing had wrapped Ethan up in its wings, its clawed hands still cupping his face, its mouth fastened to his throat. Ethan was shrivelling away beneath me, the creature sucking in all that terrible nothingness. Then the thing let go and lifted its face, casting its abyssal eyes on me.

It'll gladly take you into itself...

I scrambled up the rest of the rungs and emerged into the nave, tossing away the torch, crawling along on all fours toward the church doors. I dragged myself through them, found my feet at last and took flight, screaming, shrieking all that emptiness out of me.

The next thing I knew I was out of the graveyard, staggering around in circles under haloes of hazy streetlight. On the fringes of a housing estate I found a callbox by a lonely 24-hour kiosk. I closed myself in, leaned back into the darkness and sucked in long, steadying breaths of air.

I rummaged through my pockets for loose change. Grabbed hold of the phone receiver and punched in a number I somehow still remembered.

A familiar voice answered.

"Mum?" I said, my own voice shaking. "Mum, it's me, Violet. Sorry it's late." I swallowed a sob, wiping the tears from my face with the back of my hand. "Mum... I want to come home."

The Unseen

Chapter 1

The man behind the stall was short and rotund, with a mop of curly hair and a rounded, pockmarked face. He turned toward Lee, and Lee immediately dropped his gaze. *Jeepers Creepers. See No Evil. Saw II. Hostel.*

"Looking for anything in particular, mate?

Lee looked up and Curly-Top grinned enigmatically at him. "Not really." Lee offered a brief, cagy smile. "Just browsing, thanks."

"You into horror movies?"

Lee paused as a gust of wind snatched at his hair. "Yeah. Got anything else? Most of these don't interest me at all."

The man gestured with his thumb toward a white transit parked up behind him. "Got the obscure stuff in there, mate. Wanna look?"

The man rummaged through his pockets before Lee could reply and pulled out his van keys as he shuffled toward the vehicle. He opened the back doors to allow Lee to stick his head in.

Laid out on polythene sheets were rows and rows of DVDs, laserdiscs and videocassettes. "Got a few specialist and collector's editions in there," the man sniffed, smiling and rubbing his hands together. "Blue Underground. Anchor Bay. Alpha Video. Something Weird Video. Directors like Fulci, D'Amato, Lenzi, Mattei…"

Lee didn't hear, was too busy examining the videocassettes on display to listen. *Torture Dungeon* and *Bloodthirsty Butchers* caught his eye and, leaning forward, he quickly snatched them. "How much for these?"

The man took them from him, staring at the backs of the boxes for a while. "These are ultra-rare. Thirty quid for the pair, say?"

Lee frowned. Could he afford to spend the rest of his Job Seekers on a couple of videocassettes?

The man saw Lee was reticent, so said, quickly, "Tell you what. Thirty quid and I'll chuck in a free DVD. Can't say fairer than that, right?"

Lee carefully studied the DVD section. *Zombie Flesh Eaters. Naked Blood. Crazy Desires of a Murderer. Guinea Pig: Flower of Flesh and Blood.* Then he caught sight of himself and flinched.

"What's this?" Lee asked, grabbing hold of the DVD, staring into its mirror-effect case at a ghostly caricature of himself. "There's nothing written on the back. Not even a distribution company or anything. Looks to me like an independent feature, or home movie, maybe."

He pulled the disc out of its case and saw the words *The Black Remote* scrawled across it in black marker. "Never heard of it." He puffed out his cheeks with a deflated sigh. "Got most of the others. Guess I'll have to give this a go, then."

The man licked his lips, passed the videocassettes to Lee and closed the van doors behind him. "You come to Standerwick much?" Lee asked as he tensed against the wind.

The man smiled, shaking his head from side-to-side. "First time, mate. Come from Perranporth, Cornwall." Suddenly, the man's smile faltered and he quickly rubbed his eye with a fist. "The ending's unspeakable," he mumbled, the muscles in his face twitching. "The offerings. The Cult of the Infernal Abyss. *Synchronicity.*" He chuckled and whispered harshly into the wind. "A gate must open."

Lee felt the hairs on the back of his neck stand on end. "Eh?"

"Thirty quid," the man said, sticking out his hand and opening and closing his fingers in an impatient fashion. "Come on, come on. Haven't got all day."

Tia sat hunched on the sofa, watching *Hollyoaks* on their beat-up TV. Lee closed the door behind him and she looked up and around with accusing eyes. "Where have you been?"

He put his bag down on the floor by the coffee table and shrugged at her as he straightened. "Nowhere. Just to the market at Standerwick."

"Buy anything?"

He sucked in a breath. "Only a DVD for a couple of quid." He felt the colour rush to his cheeks. "I'm sticking the kettle on. Want a cuppa?" She shook her head, then muttered something under her breath. "What's the matter?" he asked. "What have I done this time?"

She stormed to her feet, shot over to the video cabinet and snatched open the door. "Do you remember this?" She waved a black and white

76

sleeved Sony videotape labelled *Wedding Day 2007* at him.

A thread of bile rose from the pit of his stomach, and from somewhere far off he thought he could hear screaming.

"I put it on earlier. To show Liam. You know what I got instead of images from our wedding day?" She waited futilely for an answer. "Some *crap* showing a girl getting gang-raped and then shot."

"*Last House on the Left,*" he managed, feebly. "It was showing uncut on cable a few months back. I couldn't watch it at the time because we were off out to your sister's, remember? There'd been no blank videocassettes, so I…"

"Can't believe I'm hearing this." She grimaced, baring small, stained teeth. "*That* was our wedding video, Lee. We had footage of Liam taking his first steps on it, too."

She switched the TV off, stomped across the room, and slammed the door on her way out.

Deathly silence descended.

He woke with a gasp, his face greased with sweat.

He'd fallen asleep on the sofa, the television still glowing, flickering, throwing jagged blue light across the walls.

He rubbed at his eyes, got to his feet and shuffled toward the bag full of goodies by the coffee table.

Time for a midnight movie, he thought with a grin.

He'd seen *Torture Dungeon* and *Bloodthirsty Butchers* before, so he decided on the other film, the amateurish looking one.

He stuck the DVD in, set it playing with the remote.

No credits, just a decrepit-looking house on a cliff overlooking a beach.

The sandy coves and wildflower-peppered grasslands hinted at Cornwall, which fleetingly made him think of Curly-Top back on his stall. The camera drifted upwards, where seagulls wheeled above that crumbling manse.

It cut to a darkened room.

A man in a black mask was whispering conspiratorially into the camera. Lee strained to listen, to hear, but the spoken words were difficult to make out. Slowly the camera panned through the rest of the house, revealing spiralling corridors and rooms thick with shadows and rot.

Lee discerned little in way of plot. When the narrative actually began to run, he witnessed a string of brutal murders, perpetrated by that guy in the black paper mask.

Characters were despatched moments after being introduced – some gaunt-looking guy and his girlfriend were jabbed repeatedly with a spear; a woman with pale-green eyes had her throat cut; a man in a black leather coat had his hands and feet bound by cable-wire and a plastic bag thrust over his head; a girl wearing a combat jacket was stabbed in the stomach repeatedly with a machete and finally, a scruffy-looking male was disembowelled with a butterfly knife. There were no gore effects;

the camera always panned away or the screen blacked out before it could get interesting.

Though tired, Lee found himself drawn into the film. The macabre atmosphere sang to him and the acting was of a higher calibre than usual for this type of movie.

The Black Remote (if that was what it was called – there were no credits or title sequences at the beginning or end) had no dénouement; it finished abruptly, right after the bloodless disembowelling and snow filled the screen.

The DVD timer told Lee fifty-nine minutes had elapsed; the film was short and frustratingly incomplete.

He sat there motionless, hands clasped on his knees, trying to take in what he'd seen. It had been amateurish, certainly, and he hadn't felt *scared.* Yet, on some level, the film had successfully managed to disturb him…

He rose from the sofa, made himself a cup of tea. Sat back down and searched IMDB for *The Black Remote* on his computer. No trace. He did a Google search and though he trawled through endless result pages he couldn't find any mention of the film.

The faces of the actors and actresses remained branded in his brain. Their contorted expressions, the panic in their screams…

He rubbed his chin in contemplation. Of course he didn't think the film was 'real', but he typed in 'The Black Remote snuff movie' anyway into an obscure search engine, then scrolled meticulously through the results.

This time, on the second page, he found what he thought could be a lead – the title to a thread called *The Black Remote*.

The link took him straight to a horror movie forum entitled *Let Them Die Slowly*. The forum wasn't active, had only a handful of members, but the thread was definitely called *The Black Remote*, and there was a single entry from a poster named 'Jan' on it:

Anyone seen a low-budget movie called THE BLACK REMOTE? It's a slasher set in a dilapidated Cornish mansion. Only the heavily butchered version's available, which can be found in the usual black markets across the net.

Lee pondered this for a moment or two, then signed up to the forum. He had to wait an hour for the activation email to come through, killing the time by surfing the Net.

Once the mail pinged into his inbox, he logged in and posted on *The Black Remote* thread.

I've seen it. The quality of the DVD was poor, and the movie was disjointed and amateurish. I liked the atmosphere though, and some of the acting was well above average. Unfortunately the killings occur off-camera, and so the film suffered from a lack of gore. The absence of an ending really disappointed, too.

The decayed mansion served as a memorable setting though, and I'm intrigued by the prospect of an uncut THE BLACK REMOTE – where can I find a copy?

He finished typing, then stared at the screen.

Tia surfaced in his mind abruptly, suddenly.

You know what I got instead of images from our wedding day?

He wondered if she knew he was still down here. She hated him being up so late. He dispelled the thought with a fierce shake of his head and took his empty teacup into the kitchen. His thoughts had already moved on from his wife and were now centering on the prospect of an uncensored version of *The Black Remote*. Some gore and a satisfactory ending would elevate the movie massively, he realised.

When he sat at his computer again, he noticed 'Jan' had responded to his post already.

PM me.

From the post tally next to their avatar (a faceless shadow pointing a video camera at the eye of the beholder), it was only 'Jan's' second post. Yet 'Jan' had responded straight away… which Lee thought really strange.

He clicked out the thread and brought up the members list. Selected 'Jan' and 'Send Private Message'.

Hi. PM as requested.

Lee didn't have to wait long; moments later, he received this:

The most complete version of THE BLACK REMOTE is rare and hard to obtain. However, it does tend to seek out those who are suitable... those who are worthy, shall we say?

"Huh?" Lee shook his head from side-to-side. "What's that supposed to mean?"

He glanced at the time on his computer. A quarter to five in the morning. "Christ." He vigorously knuckled his eyes. Tia would be up in an hour.

He had to get to bed. And fast.

Chapter 2

He woke to the sound of rain clattering against rooftiles.

His thoughts were scrambled, drowned in static, like snow at the end of a beaten videocassette.

He stretched out and flung back an arm. Tia's side of the bed was empty. He sat up, gazing blearily about the room. According to the clock on the dresser, it was a quarter to one in the afternoon. *"Shit."* Tia would be at work and was due to finish at four, which meant he had three hours left on his own; Tia's mum was having Liam after school so Lee could job search.

Tia had left him out a note and a newspaper cutting advertising for fork-lift truck operators in Westbury, downstairs on the kitchen table. *Saw this and thought of you. Can you pick up bread, teabags and milk at the shop. T.*

Application forms would be going out this afternoon, then the recruitment line would be closed. The job didn't interest him in the slightest, although he knew he had to find work soon; Tia's wage was barely covering the bills and their debts were mounting at a seemingly astronomical rate.

I'll ring the number, he promised, but later – he needed coffee and something to eat first.

He thought back to that message from 'Jan' as he shook cornflakes into a bowl. *The most complete version of* The Black Remote *is rare and hard to obtain.*

83

He froze and stared glassy eyed at the wall, mulling over those words. Didn't he have a reference book somewhere on obscure movies? He put the cereal box down, dashed upstairs and entered the spare bedroom.

There was a box under the bed filled with old film and horror magazines. *Fangoria. Shock Xpress. Headpress. The Dark Side. Fear.* He rummaged through them, but the book wasn't there. He opened the cupboard where a stack of books and magazines were stored and immediately a book fell and landed with a *thud* by his feet.

He stooped, picked it up.

Suddenly, the reference book fled his mind. He sat on the carpet and flicked idly through that freshly rediscovered photograph album.

There were Polaroids of Lee and Tia at parties; on holidays he could scarcely remember; of the two of them at hazily recollected social events.

In each picture he didn't recognise himself – he was smiling, his young face so fresh and alive. There were pictures of their first house together: a three-bedroomed terrace in the centre of Trowbridge. He saw faded photographs of Liam crawling; of his son in a highchair with chocolate smeared around his mouth; of his boy resting upright in the crook of Tia's arm.

The book dropped into his lap and he swiftly covered his face with his hands. Tears slid warm and silent through his fingers, spattering the plastic pockets of the album. "Sorry," he whispered to no one in particular. "So, *so* sorry."

Tia came home after five, tired, cranky and wet. Liam trudged into the house behind her, dropping his lunchbox and bag to the floor, not even bothering to acknowledge Lee as he stomped upstairs to his room.

Lee switched the TV off, hiding his *The Black Remote* DVD behind the sofa. "How was your day?"

She dumped her bags on the carpet, then said with a grimace: "Kids were a nightmare. The weather meant there was no outdoor play, so they've been cooped up inside, driving me to distraction." Tia was a teaching assistant at Roundhill Primary School, a job she disliked immensely. She found each day a struggle and never failed to return home drained. "Honestly thought I was going to lose it with them." She draped her coat over the arm of a chair before drifting silently into the kitchen.

Outside, the unrelenting rain crackled and spat against the window.

"What about the shopping?" she shouted, a short while later.

Lee squirmed in his seat. "Shit. I…"

"Bet you didn't ring about that job, either."

He chewed the inside of his mouth.

"Fuck's sake, Lee!"

He got up, clenched his fists and gingerly entered the kitchen. "Sorry."

"Don't want to hear it. Fuck off." She was seated at the table, smoking one of his cigarettes.

He couldn't think of anything else to say, so stood staring gormlessly at her for a moment or two.

85

Around him the kitchen darkened as a bare, coffin-shaped room began to superimpose itself over his surroundings…

Tia coughed, snapping him back into the present. "Have you been dipping your fingers into Liam's savings again?"

"What...?" He jumped slightly, mouth gaping open and shut as he retreated toward the door.

Her cigarette was smouldering, her thumb and forefinger almost touching as she lifted her left hand. "I'm *this* close to leaving you right now."

Panicked screams filled his skull and he shook his head to still them. Walk away, he thought. *Just walk the fuck away.*

"You're trying to distance yourself," he said quickly, not really thinking about what it was he was saying. "It's been going on for a while now. You've been turning Liam against me, too."

"How *dare* you!" Tears glistened in her eyes. "The patience I've shown, the chances I've given you!"

He whirled, grabbed his coat from off its hook in the hall. Left the house and slammed the door on his way out. He walked the estate, muttering, cursing, fists buried deep in his pockets. He didn't want to go back; not until he'd made sense of a few things first.

He wandered round in circles, occasionally pausing in the street to survey the house. Time dragged, rain seethed. Tia's shadow flitted intermittently past the living-room window.

Eventually the downstairs lights winked out and Lee counted to one hundred before making his move. He took his key out of his coat pocket, unlocked the front door and crept quietly inside. It was obvious Tia and Liam had gone to bed and so with a sigh he hung his coat on a radiator and sneaked off to the living-room to switch on his computer.

He sat at his desk, logged on to the *Let Them Die Slowly* website.

No new messages.

His shoulders sagged.

Just as he was about to log-off again, a message from 'Jan' popped up on screen, throwing him completely.

THE BLACK REMOTE is sufficiently interested in you – you have shown promise, my friend. Keep us in your thoughts, and perhaps it shall reveal itself to you soon.

Lee stared long and hard at the message, then dropped his hands into his lap and hissed, *"...the fuck?"*

Too tired to respond, too exhausted to think up a reply, he switched off the computer and rose wearily to his feet.

He caught sight of *The Black Remote* sticking out from behind the sofa.

I should go to bed, he thought. *Catch up on some sleep.*

Instead, he crouched down and scooped up the film.

Snapped open the case and fed the DVD player the disc.

Darkness reigned.

It was so thick that Lee could scarcely see his hand in front of his face.

Slowly, minutely, his eyes grew accustomed to the gloom. "I recognise this place," he whispered.

He was in a coffin-shaped room with stained walls and a grey, splintered door.

He snatched the door open and stepped out on to his own upstairs landing. He looked back to see the room had changed; was now furnished with a familiar bed, cupboard, dresser, and rug.

He gripped the stair rail and crept hesitantly down into the hall, noticing a bluish light glowing beneath the living-room door. Tentatively he approached it, freezing as he heard hoof falls and the creaking of floorboards coming from somewhere behind him.

He wheeled.

Darkness – nothing there.

"Christ." Sweating, panting, he grasped the handle and turned it until he heard the *click*. He toed the door open and entered the room.

Positioned at various points around the living-room were wax candles, flames sputtering and hissing. They were set up on the mantelpiece, the coffee table, around the TV and stereo system. The curtains had been pulled back from the window, the pane a rectangle of thick and impenetrable darkness.

Sat in an armchair in front of Lee was Tia, her blood-streaked countenance fixed and unmoving, her eyes missing from her face. Those round ragged holes glistened obscenely, and the smile she wore was the smile of a lunatic.

Liam, clad in a black paper mask, stood to her left, his head slightly bowed, his arms hanging by his sides.

Lee stepped into the room.

The boy's head shot up.

"Bywa," Liam whispered.

Lee's eyes flashed open.

"Fuck," he gasped, straightening, hastily wiping a thread of drool from off his chin. *"Fuck!"* His heart thudded and thundered, cold sweat beaded his brow.

The TV was humming and flickering in the corner. He stood, disorientated, then realised he'd fallen asleep on the sofa again.

"Dad?"

Lee twitched and whirled toward the voice. Liam, dressed in his Superman pyjamas and cape, was lingering in the living-room doorway. Something like relief flowed through Lee when he saw his boy was unmasked and that his eyeballs were most definitely intact. "Liam, hi. Hi. What…?"

"You were dreaming." Liam tilted his head to one side. "Talking and shouting in your sleep again."

"Was I?" Lee emitted a brittle, nervous-sounding laugh. "You okay? Where's Mum?"

"She's out, remember? Visiting Aunt Trudie. She left early. Didn't want to disturb you."

89

They were silent for a moment. Then, softly, Liam said, "Mum said to wake you at nine. I've got football practice, remember?"

"I remember."

Liam nodded once, turned, and hurried upstairs to his room.

They left for football practice a short while later.

They scurried through teeming rain, their hoods raised, their coats zipped up to their throats. Lee knew it was selfish, but all he wanted was to curl up somewhere and watch movies all day. He tried not to show his resentment, even tried to seem interested in the early stages of the training session.

During a five-a-side match, Lee lingered on the side lines as the other fathers screamed and gesticulated wildly at their sons. He stood hunched and grim-faced, the rain hammering down around him.

In his head, Lee was inside a coffin-shaped room in a dark and decayed mansion…

He rubbed his eyes quickly.

Overhead, apocalyptic clouds gathered into shapes, figures, faces. He felt wheezy and out of breath, had to turn away from the other fathers so that they wouldn't notice.

Was he having a heart attack?

He stumbled into the Sport's Hall to get himself some water. He found the fountain and quickly drank his fill. When he re-emerged, moments later, the referee blew for full-time and the two teams trudged off the field toward their waiting

90

parents. Some of the kids went to the hall to shower, but Liam wanted to go home and change.

"Did you see me?" Liam asked, clapping his hands, his mud-spattered face projecting the most incredible grin. "Did you see me score the winner, Dad?"

Lee, unsettled and disturbed, stared blankly at him.

They walked home, neither speaking.

Liam hitched his bag over his shoulder, eyes not leaving the ground. The grin was gone, his metal studs scraping the pavement as he walked. Lee, desperately trying to think of something to say, clutched at his coat and stared long and hard into the middle distance.

They arrived at the house a short while later. Liam took his boots off outside, then ran wordlessly upstairs. Tia – back early from Trudie's – looked up and around at Lee from her chair in the corner. "How was it?"

Liam slammed the bathroom door, and Lee winced.

"Is he okay?" Tia's eyes were hard and unblinking. "What happened?"

"Nothing. It went well. He scored the winner." Lee purposely changed the subject. "How's Trudie?"

"Fine." Her slender shoulders dropped a fraction. "She's invited us over for dinner tomorrow."

"I can't do that," he said, surprising himself.

Her expression crumpled. "Why not?"

91

"Because I don't like being around people, Tia. I'm…struggling. Sorry."

For some reason Curly-Top flashed into his mind, grinning that odd, enigmatic grin. Then he was back in the moment when she said, softly, "I don't know what's got into you, I really don't. It's like I don't know you anymore."

Without warning she got up and left the room, leaving him exposed to a stark and uneasy silence.

"I'm standing on the edge of something." The words spewed from his lips like bile. "This is *mine*. Something for me."

He fell to his knees and switched on the TV. Fed the DVD player *The Black Remote*.

That decrepit house loomed. The camera panned down long, eerie corridors.

Shadows moved indelibly in corners.

Curved blades glinted and fell.

During the scene where the fourth victim – the guy in the leather coat – descends into a subterranean chamber, Lee thought he saw a shape in the corner of the screen, a hunched figure with horns sprouting from its head.

Now he was beginning to understand what he liked about the film – you could never trust what it was you were seeing…

The killer stepped out of the darkness with the mask over his face and whispered something – two words – into the camera.

Lee patted around for the controller, grabbed it. Rewound and re-played it.

Coaxed the killer out of the shadows again.

"Asterion House."

There. That was it.

He left the video frozen on that black-masked face, hurried across the room and switched his computer on.

It took searching through endless result pages to find mention of the house and the link took him straight to a website on derelict buildings and abandoned places.

A grainy photograph of *Asterion House* appeared – the same house featured in *The Black Remote*, there could be no doubting it.

There were a few words written about the house underneath the picture:

This dilapidated mansion on the East Pentire headland overlooks Crantock Beach and the Gannel Estuary, which runs from the river mouth in Crantock Bay along the edge of Newquay.

Abandoned during the nineteenth century, little is known about its previous inhabitants, although they were believed to have been a family of influence and high social standing. The last in line was a recluse, who rarely left...

Lee scrolled down to see photographs of some of the interior rooms...and recognised them immediately.

One of the photographs depicted the coffin-shaped room where the characters had met their grisly demises. *So they actually shot the film inside the house,* Lee thought with a shudder.

There was something chalked on the floor in the coffin-shaped room and, by pressing his face

93

close to the monitor, he discerned a five-pointed star inside a circle.

His window closed down suddenly and he was left staring at his desktop. He tried retrieving the page, but was met with the error message: 'This website is currently not available'.

Muttering under his breath, he logged on to *Let Them Die Slowly* and found a message from 'Jan' in his inbox.

He clicked on it, frowned.

Re-read it with a curious mixture of excitement and disbelief:

You have been invited to a special screening of the most complete version of THE BLACK REMOTE at Asterion House tomorrow evening. I shall meet you outside Newquay Railway Station at precisely 6 PM.

I sincerely look forward to meeting you in person. You are very lucky to have been chosen, my friend.

Chapter 3

Lee feigned sleep while Tia got herself and Liam dressed. He didn't stir until he heard the front door slam. Then he got himself dressed, took £25 out of Liam's piggy bank and made the long walk to the train station on the other side of town.

He carefully planned his route by the timetable in the ticket office, boarding his first train shortly before noon. There was just one change at Bristol Parkway; after that it was a straight run, getting him to Newquay at a quarter to six in the evening.

Throughout his journey, his thoughts alternated wildly between Tia and *The Black Remote*. He was excited by the prospect of watching the most-complete version of a movie few had seen before, but that was tempered by the guilt of embarking on the journey in the first place. He'd left a note for Tia explaining all, yet he knew she wouldn't understand; this was something for *him*, something he could finally call his own. Once it was over, he would turn his sole and undivided attention to his family again.

I'll be a better man, he thought. *Like the me in those photographs I found the other day.*

He arrived in Newquay dead on time.

He stepped off the train, took his mobile from his jacket and scanned it for messages and missed calls. Why hadn't Tia been in contact? She must have seen his note by now. He put the phone away just as a hand gripped his arm and turned him.

"You're Lee, aren't you?" He stood facing a man in a shabby grey suit and tie. The man's mouth twitched inside a dishevelled beard. "You've come for *The Black Remote,* right?"

Lee nodded.

"Jan." The man offered Lee his hand, which Lee timidly shook. "Nice to meet you. This way please." Jan turned smartly toward a silver Mercedes parked close to a taxi rank, opening the passenger door for Lee to sidle inside.

Jan slipped into the vehicle, pulled on his seatbelt and started up the engine. "We haven't far to go. Strap yourself in, please."

Jan pulled away and soon they were easing along a quiet coastal road, the car's headlights lancing through the darkness. The night smothered the scenery; there was nothing to be seen beyond the twisting, winding surface of the road.

"I'm glad you liked the film." Jan's voice resonated throughout the car, untangling Lee from his thoughts. "It's been such a long and arduous shoot."

Lee frowned and glared at Jan's reflection hovering in the darkness of the windscreen. "Where are we?"

"Crantock." Jan's fingers visibly tightened around the wheel. "We're almost there. The house has stood on the cliff overlooking the estuary for hundreds of years. Used to overlook Langarrow, too."

"Langarrow?" Lee was only half-listening; a remote part of him was desperately trying to make itself heard, instructing him to stop, to turn back, to flee this madness immediately.

"Langarrow used to exist between Crantock and Perran," Jan said with a stiff nod of his head. "Until the sands buried it, of course. Wrath of God, they said." He laughed humourlessly, then said with a smirk: "Some great men lived in Langarrow. Before the storm it was a city of vice, populated by convicts shipped in or trucked across from less...*tolerant* places. My Master's followers built the house on the cliff overlooking the city and that's how it's survived to this very day. My fellow brethren and I have been ensconced beneath the house for a good many years, working tirelessly to bring our Master's vision to life..."

They were slowing down, pulling up in front of some wrought-iron gates.

Jan cranked the handbrake, then operated the electric window. It slid down smoothly and he reached out a veiny hand to press a button on the gatepost.

With the car idling, Lee gazed at distant lights shimmering like an alien constellation on the horizon. "Holiday parks," Jan sniffed, noticing his interest. "A travesty really, considering what was there once."

The gates shuddered open and Jan released the handbrake. Lee's nose wrinkled as the sulphuric smell of the estuary infiltrated the car; with a grimace he swallowed down his nausea and focused on the windscreen.

Dishevelled trees brushed against the Mercedes. Thorny branches scratched at its roof.

The car jolted and shuddered as it passed over potholes, knocking Lee from side to side, Jan's reflection flickering like a trapped frame on a screen before him. Then, rising out of the night, grey stone, rotted wood and cracked tiles became starkly illuminated by the headlights.

"Asterion House," Lee whispered with awe.

Jan pulled up outside the doors and then cut the car's engine. He jumped out, came round to Lee's side and opened the passenger door. Lee clambered out, squinting at the house as he straightened.

Wrought-iron balustrades and wooden decking hung broken, twisted and askew. Windows were black, sightless eyes. Unintelligible graffiti scarred the brickwork and the neglected outbuildings around them.

Jan hurried toward the doors, fitted a key in the lock and turned it. "So glad you could join us. Especially tonight of all nights!" He pushed and the doors rumbled ominously open. "January 27th. St Winebald's Day! The perfect time to screen *The Black Remote*, don't you think?" He turned and grinned, beckoning Lee in with a finger. "You'll meet the rest of the house later, I promise. But first, let's go enjoy the film, eh?"

Unanswered questions rippled through Lee's mind as he followed the man through the doorway into a cavernous hall. Candles burned in glass jars. Cobwebs shrouded skewed chandeliers. To their right a staircase curled away into darkness; without hesitation Jan ascended, his feet thudding down on the wooden treads.

The stairs led to a darkened landing where an unpainted door awaited. "In here," Jan said, twisting and pushing the handle, "is the theatre." The door opened onto red swing seats and a whirring projector set behind a window in an adjacent wall. The room was only partially lit by the projector's pale-blue glow and a red EXIT sign buzzing on the wall opposite.

Lee felt too on edge to fully appreciate the cinema's dank and decayed charm and so lingered in the darkness for a while, spellbound and silent.

"Take a pew," Jan said and Lee snapped from his reverie as Jan brushed past him to shuffle along the third row of seats from the front. Jan stopped, pulled open a chair and perched himself on it. Lee sat beside him, crushing his hands together in his lap.

A blank screen suddenly filled the wall before them, followed by exterior images of Asterion House. Moments later shots of empty rooms flashed before Lee's eyes. He blinked and looked around curiously, scanning the room for others, but there was nobody here but them.

He grimaced, his eyes flicking back to the movie.

The man in the black paper mask stepped out of the darkness toward the camera, *toward the viewer* and Lee felt himself shudder involuntarily.

The thin-looking male and his dark-haired girlfriend squealed and shrieked as they were jabbed repeatedly with the spear; the woman with pale-green eyes gurgled horribly as blood spurted from her open throat; the plastic, vomit-clotted bag sucked in tight around the young man's face as he fought futilely against his ties; the girl in the combat jacket pleaded convincingly for her life before the machete was plunged into her; finally, the scruffy-looking male emitted a harrowing scream as his belly was slashed, his innards slopping out of that cavity to land steaming by his feet.

Thoughts of snuff movies again surfaced and Lee gripped the armrests to still his trembling hands.

It's not one of those, he told himself. *Just fucking good acting and effects.*

After the final kill, Jan stood abruptly and made his way toward the centre aisle, his seat swinging shut behind him.

Lee barely noticed, his eyes still glued to the screen.

Will I be rewarded with an ending this time? he thought with a frisson of excitement. To his disappointment the movie blacked out and snow filled the screen, just like it had done on DVD. "Where's my ending?" he whispered, turning in his seat to look about him again.

The chairs were empty; of his host there was no sign.

He left his seat, hurried toward the door they'd entered by. Grabbed the handle and turned it.

Locked.

"Let me out!" he shouted, shaking the handle violently. "Open the *fucking* door!"

No reply.

The projector whirred and the film suddenly restarted, exterior shots of Asterion House giving way to rooms thick with cobwebs, shadow and rot.

Lee made his way over to the EXIT sign, discovering a small door beneath it. He grabbed the handle, throwing one last look over his shoulder as he turned it.

Someone was standing behind the window next to the projector – a tall, stooped silhouette with an elephantine head and torso.

Lee cursed as he stumbled out of that grim auditorium, leaving the door open behind him. He was in a corridor now, narrow and oppressively dark. He slipped his mobile out of his pocket and used its meagre light to see.

In front of him were steps leading down into a deep damp vault.

The door slammed.

He wheeled, hearing a key scrape loudly in the lock. "Hey!" he shouted, reaching for the handle, rattling it hard. "Let me out! Let me out, you *fuck!* What the *fuck's* going on here, *eh?*" His voice echoed off stone walls and gradually faded to nothingness. With a snort of self-loathing, he vehemently rubbed tears from his eyes and cautiously approached the stairs.

He placed one foot in front of the other, descending into a chamber lit by candles in small alcoves. Directly in front of him was a splintered door, hanging ajar as though ready to receive him.

He checked his phone again, considered calling the police. He could alert them to what was going on; direct them to Asterion House and the secret

101

rooms inside it. But as he lifted his mobile, he swore under his breath – no signal.

A low chuckle.

He spun to see something red flashing in the gloom.

Rather than confront whoever was there, Lee snatched open the door and stumbled into the familiar confines of a cold, coffin-shaped room…

More candles burned and dripped in the darkness, and shadows twitched and slithered across bare, filth-encrusted walls.

Before him, chalked in red on warped floorboards, was a five-pointed star and around it – within the wide outer circle – were the six victims of *The Black Remote*.

They stood facing one another, frozen at the consummate moment; on the very brink of death.

In the far corner of the room, a group of robed figures whispered amongst themselves as Lee edged nervously forward. He ignored them, eyes locking on the stars of *The Black Remote* instead.

The boyfriend and girlfriend with their torn, ruptured flesh.

The young man with plastic pulled tight around his face.

The woman with the pale-green eyes clutching at her throat.

The girl with the machete embedded in her body.

The scruffy, unshaven male bent over, his stomach eviscerated.

They looked horribly lifelike – too authentic to be anything but… *real*. "My God."

He had to at least try and phone the police, try and get help and, ripping his phone out of his pocket, he saw he had signal at last.

He hit 999 with trembling fingers, but his mobile rang before he could make the call. He held the device up, Tia's number flashing before him. He dropped it as he attempted to answer, the phone bouncing, spinning and skittering away across the room.

One of the robed figures snatched it up, candlelight painting the pockmarked face within the hood.

"He's here, with us. The Cult of the Infernal Abyss." Curly-Top pressed the phone closer to his sneering lips. "Thank you for all you've done. The boy, too."

Lee's attention was snatched toward another figure – the black-masked man – who'd stepped out of an alcove and was now wielding a chainsaw in his hands. He was giggling, staring intently over Lee's shoulder at something. "Ready, Master?"

The masked man yanked the chainsaw cord and Lee shrank toward the door, then whirled when he heard hoof falls and the creaking of floorboards.

There was that flashing again – a tiny red dot – and Lee realised he was looking straight into the lens of a video camera.

The operator lingered near the open door, Lee catching sight of fur-lined shins and cloven hooves.

He spun to face the chainsaw again, which had now gunned into life.

"Watch!" the masked man shouted as he raised the saw above his head. "Watch and *marvel,* friend!" He nodded toward the half-dead things positioned around the star. "Bywa!"

Those things instantly came to life, shrieking and squealing in their death throes.

"Rewi!"

The word stilled them, denying them death once more.

Within those ragged holes, the masked man's eyes widened above his saw as he said, loudly, "We're almost there. *Almost.* We've been searching for the right formula for *centuries.* Now it's just you … the last of the seven … and it has to be *simultaneous!* All of you at the same time. To bring this to an end – so that *many* can witness *The Black Remote* in its full and flagrant glory!"

The words barely registered as Lee recognised that deep, booming voice as Jan's. He shook the realisation off and looked for an escape route, but an abrupt swipe from Jan's saw forced him between those half-dead things in the circle. With a cry he attempted to punch the man, but the saw dropped and bit deep into Lee's arm, blood spurting off in all different directions.

The robed figures in the corner laughed pitilessly at his plight.

Above the sound of his own screams, Lee heard Jan shout "Bywa!" and immediately the other victims came to life, shuddering and shaking as they rushed inexorably toward oblivion.

The saw dropped again, ploughing straight into Lee's chest, sending him sprawling to the ground before his attacker's feet.

Jan cut his saw and tore off his mask, his bearded face twitching with delight. "The gate's opening." He turned toward the misshapen figure with the camera. Looked again at Lee and the red pentagram on the floor. "The Spawn of the Abyss will bring blessed insanity to all!" His voice quivered on the verge of hysteria.

Blood was erupting from Lee, his vision fading, breaking, failing. The other victims collapsed like string-severed marionettes, their blood staining the floorboards, their mouths wide and grotesque Os.

The Master cantered forward, camera raised, filming the smoke that was beginning to billow and rise all around them. Suddenly Jan's eyes bulged, and he laughed and screamed at the same time. The robed figures in the corner began to scream too, and raising their hands they clawed frantically at their faces until bubbling pools of crimson had replaced their eyes.

The Master continued shooting as Lee felt the presence of many begin to materialise around him. And as he tried to turn, to see them, total darkness descended before he could catch so much as a glimpse of his ending.

Home

Mum and Carl were in the kitchen, talking to somebody I didn't recognise. The official was tall and lean, with a tanned, tear-shaped face. An ID card displaying a miniaturised version of that same face hung around his neck, crocodile-clipped to a lanyard.

"Once a year," he said, "the veil between worlds wears so thin that…"

I withdrew into the lounge, fixing my gaze on the wingback chair by the window. Sometimes I can still picture Dad there, smoking and drinking neat whisky, black threads from his cigarette coiling upwards, upwards.

A blur of movement snapped me from my thoughts. I looked up to see Will, dressed in faded jeans and a hoodie, crossing the road outside the window.

The kitchen door squeaked as it widened, the man declaring, "…about fear, or *controlling* it. That's what he'll feed on. That's what he wants from you all."

I edged back into the hall, my hands crushed together in front of me.

"The first time is always the worst," the man said, stepping out of the kitchen with a small suitcase in his hand. "And I can tell it's been hanging over you all for some time. Don't let it spoil the good you have here." He nodded at me. "She's worth fighting for. They both are."

He left us at last, closing the front door behind him, me, Mum and Carl taking ourselves off into the quiet of the lounge.

Mum was silent for a while. Then, following my gaze to our father's chair, she put her hands on her hips and said, "Can't believe how stupid I've been. I should've made the room less familiar for him."

Carl grabbed hold of the chair, turning it and pushing it away into the corner of the room. "When we have the money," he said, straightening, smiling weakly, "we'll replace it. About time we had a refurbish, right?"

I know Carl makes Mum feel safe. Makes us all feel safe, I suppose. He doesn't have to be here, not really. Someday I hope to feel comfortable enough to call him Dad.

"Where's Will?" Mum asked, a sudden tinge of fear in her voice. "It's getting late. He should be home."

She looked at me and I shrugged, not letting on that I'd seen him just now. "Don't worry," I said, snatching my coat from off the back of the sofa. "I'll find him."

"Be careful." Panic flashed through her eyes. "You can say the man's gone, if that's what's been bothering him."

I opened the door and hurried outside, streetlamps winking on around me. I shoved my hands in my pockets, stalking the lanes and back alleys of the estate, calling his name. Between blocks of mouldering terraces, I watched the sunset spread its fire across town.

Clustered in a black doorway was a family of four—father, mother, son and daughter—their faces powdered white and their eyes rimmed with kohl. They smiled at me as I passed. There was a banner reading WELCOME HOME taped to the brickwork above their heads. Tea-lights burned on the windowsill, positioned between gaudy papier-mâché skulls, charms and other esoteric trinkets.

I quickened my pace, food packets and wrappers blowing about my ankles. I leapt over a crumbling stone wall and crouched amongst briars and weeds, a crooked spire cutting into the sky above.

Between skewed black railings I saw his face through twilight's accreting layers. There were others here, too, but they kept separate vigils; waiting and watching, they wanted to be the first to greet their dead.

I unlatched the gate, stepped around it and entered the graveyard. Will was sitting at Dad's grave, a wicked looking knife on his lap.

I crouched by his side. "Come home," I breathed.

"Home?" His gaze lifted and focused on the granite slab which bore our father's name. "Nowhere's home, Sylvie."

I noticed his hands were clenched, his brows knotted together. I reached out, gently shaking him. "Hate won't change a thing. Remember what the man said?"

"Fuck the suits and the social workers," he hissed. "*They* can't stop him from coming."

108

I managed to shape my mouth into a smile. "But *we* need you. And if we're going to get through this…" I paused mid-sentence, watching the tears flow quickly down his face.

"I *look* like him, Sylvie. I share his fucking DNA."

"You're *nothing* like him." I took hold of his face, turning him toward me. "You don't have his eyes, right? Look—you have Mum's eyes. You're not like him at all."

"But he always knew how to get inside me." He shoved me away, wiping the tears from his cheeks with the sleeve of his hoodie. "Remember Benji?"

A year ago, when Dad was still alive, Will'd smashed a bottle of whisky; in retaliation, Dad had killed our pet dog by stringing it up by its neck with the belt he used to hit us with.

"Will." I touched his hand and his face screwed up into a grimace. "I hate him, too. The nights I lay there, scared, waiting for…"

"I should've known," he spat. "Should have realised. I could have stopped…"

"None of it's *your* fault." I wrapped my arm around his shoulders. "What matters is you're here *now*. For me. Mum, too."

"But I'm frightened about what he can do. *Still* do."

"You're strong, Will…"

"I'm not strong, Sylvie." He shoved me again and clambered to his feet, collecting up his knife. Together, we staggered out of the graveyard and made our way homewards.

Mum met us at the front door. "You're back," she gasped. "Thank God you're back." Will managed to conceal his knife from her beneath the front of his hoodie sweatshirt. In the lounge, Carl was standing by the window, peering out at people gathering in the street, lanterns and candle flames bobbing like will-o'-the-wisps in the darkness.

Mum sucked in a breath. "I'll make a start on supper, eh?"

Will dashed upstairs before anyone could stop him.

"Will!" Mum cried. "*Please.* We should…"

Carl seized her arm. "It's enough that he's here. Let him be, love."

Mum nodded, perched herself on the sofa, and quietly muttered, "Suppose all we can do now is wait."

Carl pulled the curtains along their runners, screening the outside world from view. I paced the room, my thoughts all over the place. Moments later, I went upstairs to check on Will.

His bedroom door was ajar. I peered through the gap and saw him sitting on his bed, the knife still lying on his lap. I knocked, calling out his name. He looked up and around, shadows falling across his face.

"I *want* him real," he growled. "I want to hurt him, Sylvie."

"But that'll give him what he wants, remember?"

He swore under his breath, leapt to his feet and closed the door in my face, leaving me all alone on the landing.

Down in the kitchen, Mum had pulled on her grey, woollen cardigan. "It's gotten so very cold in here," she said. She shifted on her stool and held her hands out to me, and I sat on her lap, letting her pull me in close. "If you hear him," she whispered, "don't listen to a word he says. Don't give him the satisfaction, okay?"

Carl switched the radio on, but it immediately turned itself off again. He glanced around, confusion stamped across his features. I pretended it hadn't happened and pressed my ear to Mum's chest, listening to the sound of her rapidly accelerating heartbeat.

I felt a hand on my shoulder, stubble scraping my cheek.

"Promise we'll be alone again soon, Sylvie."

I shrieked and recoiled, Mum enveloping me with her arms, holding and squeezing me tight. I was gasping and shaking, aware of the stench of whisky and cigarette smoke carrying in the air.

"He's here," I cried. "He was right beside me!"

Will charged downstairs, his eyes wide and startled looking. We met him in the lounge just as our father's chair scraped across the floor toward us.

Dad's face began to form, white and luminous, flickering, sneering above the wingback chair.

Will saw it and immediately pulled the knife from behind his back.

"No." I stepped forward, putting my hand on Will's arm.

The leering visage wavered and shimmered, surrounded by flickering wisps of ethereal fog.

Carl seized Will's shoulders, turning him, steering him out the room and into the hall. "It won't do a thing, Will," he whispered. Will's head was lowered, his breath coming in ragged, uneven gasps. It wasn't just Will—we were all scared; thoughts of this night and what it might bring have been eating away at us for months.

I raised my head to see Dad sink into his chair, an awful grin materialising on his face. He looked like he was composed of mist, his body swirling and reconstituting every time he moved. He opened his mouth, emitting brays of horrible, echoey laughter.

"Go away," I snarled. Fuck off and leave us alone. We're not leaving because of you. Not tonight, not ever.

Me and Mum clutched at each other, trying to show him we were strong, that he couldn't break us. We closed our eyes, not wanting to see him, to even acknowledge his presence. The ensuing minutes felt like hours. *You're not here,* I kept thinking. *There's only me, Mum, Will and Carl. We're family. A force to be reckoned with.*

Eventually a kind of stillness, a wave of peace, descended and we reopened our eyes, our bodies sweating despite the cold.

"Is he…?" Mum glanced around, eyes drawn to the wingback chair once more. She shivered and wrapped her arms around herself. Will shuffled back into the room, the knife gone and his gaze nailed to the floor. He still looked so pale and jittery, I thought.

112

We could hear whoops and shouting coming from the street, but it was different here. Was always going to be, I suppose.

Had he *really* passed through?

My heart rate began to slow and I felt much less anxious, much less afraid.

Will made for the stairs.

"Will…" Mum said, her head snapping up. *"Stay. Please."*

"It's okay." He tried placating her with a smile. "He's gone. He must have. Everything's normal again, right?"

Carl was by Mum's side now, gripping her hand, stroking her knuckles. Mum watched Will traipse upstairs, her expression telling me she was still concerned about him.

I perched on the sofa, listening to the hollers, shrieks and cheers coming from the celebrants outside. It sounded all so alienating, all so unreal.

Mum and Carl retired to the kitchen to make coffee. The temperature felt normal, the house still again.

I rose, making for the stairs.

"Sylvie?" Mum called.

"Just checking on Will," I said.

"Ask him to come down, love."

I found him in the bathroom, squinting and staring at his features in the mirror above the sink. *I look like him.*

It was bright in there, the strip light casting its stark luminescence onto his face. By his sides, his hands were screwed up into tight, trembling balls. "Will?"

113

His eyes rolled in my direction, his countenance flickering, as if another face was trying to overlay itself on top.

I stepped back, startled. He lunged around me, closing the door before I could flee. His eyes were a different colour, I realised. Cigarette smoke and whisky fumes rode on his breath.

"Promised we'd be alone again," he hissed and, as Will's anguished, screaming features appeared and then disappeared, his hands unclenched and reached for me.

Out Of Hiding

Aaron crouched beside the spider's web, scowling, grimacing at it. He flicked the spark wheel of his lighter, holding the flame close. The web swiftly began to shrivel and shrink, blackening toward the creature at its centre.

The patio door slid open. "What *are* you doing?" Leanne asked, fractiously.

The spider dropped to the ground, righted itself and scurried off beneath the fence.

Aaron straightened, sliding his lighter into the front pocket of his jacket. She glared and glared as though she expected him to do something, say something. Instead, feeling stupid and small, he averted his gaze toward the overgrown grass in their garden.

More webs glinted in the sunlight.

***

Aaron stumbled into the house, wet through from rain. He took off his shoes and folded his coat over the radiator to dry.

He heard faint, giggly voices coming from the front room. Leanne had invited her friend, Sharon, around for the afternoon, he remembered, suddenly. He drifted into the kitchen, swigged from an open bottle of Merlot. He didn't want to go into the front room; didn't like Sharon, or the way Leanne changed whenever she was around her.

The door to the front room stood ajar. Aaron went toward it, bottle in hand, listening.

"How did you feel when you heard?"

"Weird. It was *so* long ago. Yet in some ways, it feels like only yesterday."

Aaron shrank back toward the fridge. He opened its door and helped himself to a piece of leftover chicken. Made a point of slamming the door shut after.

"Aaron?" Leanne called. "You home?"

"Yes," he said then mumbled under his breath, "who else were you expecting?"

He turned from the fridge just as a spider came scuttling out from under the table, disappearing into the gap beneath the cooker. It was large and fat, with a distinctive white streak on its back.

Aaron gulped more wine, put the bottle down, then reluctantly made for the front room.

Leanne and Sharon stopped giggling as soon as he entered.

"Hi, Sharon." He waved stiffly at her.

"Hi, Aaron."

"How was work?" Leanne asked.

"Same old, same old."

He stood in silence, trying to think of something else to say. Leanne looked bemused, almost embarrassed for him. "I'm going to go dry off," he said at last.

Leanne nodded, "Sure." Then, as he was leaving, added: "We were talking about organising a party. I was thinking we could have it here."

"Sounds great," he lied, passing through the door, closing it behind him and heading sullenly for the stairs.

***

Later that evening, as they lay in bed together, Leanne turned to him and asked, "You okay?"

He lowered his Kindle, glancing warily up at her. "Why wouldn't I be?"

"You seem quiet. Tense, even."

Something twitched and scratched restlessly at the back of his skull. He set his Kindle down on the duvet. "I'm knackered," he said. "I'll feel better if I get my eight hours in, I'm sure."

She turned her attention back to her phone, tapping the screen with her finger.

"Who you messaging?" he asked.

She turned her phone toward herself so he couldn't see. "No one. Friends. About the party we're going to have next Friday."

He hitched the covers up around his shoulders, then shifted his body away from her. She muttered something, but he didn't hear, wasn't bothered by what she had to say.

Something caught his attention beyond the open bedroom door, something as big as a fist, crouched down in a wedge of light cast by a streetlamp outside.

It had a white streak on its back. Long, prickly legs. Twitching and bristling, growing steadily before his eyes.

Aaron buried his head beneath his pillow. Should he say something? No—he felt too awkward, too embarrassed to broach it with Leanne.

When he looked again, the thing had gone. He knew it wouldn't have gotten very far.

He needed to confront it, he realised. Kill it. Before it could get any bigger.

***

Aaron and Leanne took their usual morning stroll into town on Saturday, squeezing and bustling their way through the crowds.

They entered a café, chose a table beneath a print of Van Gogh's *The Starry Night*. They took off their coats, folded them over the backs of the chairs. Sat down and waited in silence to be served.

Aaron remembered a time when they used to enjoy chatting. These days they seemed to have so very little to talk about.

They drank their lattes and ate brioches smeared with butter and jam. People jostled and squirmed past the windows. She mentioned the party again, which irked. Said quite a few of their friends were coming. Aaron had few friends of his own. The ones he did have he shared with Leanne, who liked her better than him, he felt.

She set her coffee mug down on the table. "You didn't need to come out, Aaron. If you're feeling unwell, you should've stayed home."

"I'm okay," he sniffed. "It's just so busy out. Overwhelming, you know?"

"Why don't you go for a run when we get back? You always feel better after a run."

They gathered up their coats and paid the bill a short while later. They were pulling open the door when a man stepped up to come through. He had slicked-back hair with a white streak running through it. He looked surprised when he saw Leanne. "Leanne?" he said. "My God!" He laughed brightly, beaming from ear-to-ear. "Wow, it's been so long."

She laughed, too, clearly flustered because her cheeks and throat had flushed red. "Simon," she said. "You're back."

He stepped outside as they did, lingering under the café's wide canopy. He pushed his hands into his pockets, rocking backwards and forwards on his heels. "It's funny how things work out. Or don't, in my case."

"It's great to see you again," Leanne smiled.

"You too."

"Were you just going in?"

"Was going to grab a coffee. This place any good?"

"Best café in town." She glanced round at Aaron. "Oh, this is Aaron. Aaron, meet Simon." Simon smiled awkwardly and held out his hand. Aaron shook it, briefly. "We go way back, Simon and I."

Aaron smiled, but couldn't bring himself to say anything.

"I got your invitation," Simon said.

Leanne beamed. "Great. You coming?"

"Yeah. It'll be cool to see everyone again."

"Fantastic." She giggled self-consciously, twirling her hair around her forefinger. "See you Friday, then."

He nodded. "Looking forward to it."

Simon raised his hand and gave a departing wave, then pushed through the door into the café. The colour slowly shrank from Leanne's face.

"Who's he?" Aaron asked as they dodged down a side street to avoid the crowds.

"An old friend." She zipped her jacket up to her throat. "There was a group of us. We used to hang out all the time." She chewed her lip as if deliberating over what to say next. "You'll like him," she said, eventually.

They didn't speak again until they arrived home. It was Leanne's turn to withdraw; he couldn't even begin to imagine what she was thinking about. Or perhaps he could—ideas formed inside his mind that he didn't like so much.

Soon she started talking about the party again—what they needed to buy; how the house could be rearranged; where they could put people up if they decided to sleep over. Aaron had had enough. He told her he was going for that run, got changed and left.

***

Two nights before the party he experienced a strange and unsettling dream. He was on his way to the party, walking along an empty street toward his house. He felt inexplicably anxious, worrying over how he might impress Leanne.

120

He reached the front door, rapped loudly with his knuckles. Leanne opened it, blinking, smiling at him. "Aaron," she said. "How lovely to see you." She was wearing the dress he liked her in, the black one with the V neck and tassels. She beckoned him in. He heard music playing from the front room. It was a song he knew Leanne loved, but he hated—a generic pop number whose title eluded him. Guests were talking and laughing in the front room, but whenever he tried to look at them, he saw only their shadows, fluttering and flickering across the walls.

"Have you met Simon?" Leanne asked and then Simon appeared behind her, his arms wrapped around her waist. The white streak in his hair appeared more prominent and he grinned at Aaron as she said: "We go way back, Simon and I."

Aaron noticed Simon's face was convulsing, like there was something under the skin trying to break out…

Aaron gasped awake, rising, coughing and spluttering. Leanne sat up, too. She put the flat of her hand on his spine, rubbing it in soft, circular motions. "You okay? Whatever's the matter?"

His jaw was aching, pain tearing up both sides of his face. He rubbed his jaw, wondering if he'd been grinding his teeth again.

He cast back the duvet, tramped downstairs. Filled the kettle and snatched a mug from out of the cupboard over the sink. The sun was beginning its ascent, through the window it was painting the kitchen walls with its fiery hue.

Leanne joined him at their dining table a short while later, wrapped in her dressing gown and with her hair hanging in dishevelled ribbons in front of her face.

"Do you want some coffee?" he asked.

She shook her head.

He touched his jaw again. "My face aches like fuck. My jaw hurts, all around here. I feel sick, too."

"I'm worried about you," she said. "Sounds like a symptom of stress to me. I really think you should make a doctor's appointment."

He ran a finger around the rim of his coffee mug.

"I rang your Mum the other day," she said and he looked up in surprise. "She told me about your…phobias, shall we say? How they developed into delusions, Aaron. Things got bad when your parents split, right?" He didn't know what to say to that; he just kept quiet, staring at his hands clasped together in his lap.

She flashed him a sad, tired smile. "I know you had help before. Perhaps it's worth you seeking some again?"

Suddenly, she was exasperated by his silence.

"It's you," she snapped. "The poison in your body and mind, polluting the landscape! It's not the outside world at all; you're perfectly safe, you know. You're your own worst enemy, you always were."

He wasn't even sure if he was hearing her properly—it could quite easily be his mother speaking, not Leanne at all.

Leanne rose and swept out of the kitchen, slamming the door behind her. Her words had washed over him. He hadn't seen the thing in days.

But he knew what it was.

Knew where it was hiding, too.

***

"Help me move this, Aaron." It was the afternoon of the party. Aaron joined Leanne in the utilities room and together they cleared a stack of items from off the floor: a sack of charcoal; a rusted bicycle; a bottle of lighter fluid; a crate of old books. Aaron squeezed and sidled past her, then lifted and carried a table out to the front room.

"Do you think we'll need the other one?" Leanne asked, glancing at the second fold-out table standing up against the wall in the corner.

"If we need it," Aaron called, "I'll grab it later, okay?"

They were soon locked in their own separate worlds, Leanne rearranging the furniture, Aaron cooking and preparing the food out in the kitchen. He wasn't afraid, he realised; he knew its plans and intentions. He mustn't keep letting these things scuttle away from him because they only came back bigger and uglier in the end.

When people began arriving, Aaron kept busy prepping the food, pouring drinks, washing up after himself, which pissed Leanne off immensely. At one point he glanced down at the space between floor and cooker and remembered when it had been small enough to hide in there. Not now, though.

He carried serving platters and bowls of nibbles on a tray into the front room. Leanne, Sharon and Simon were standing in a corner, laughing at something Simon had said. Leanne was reaching up to touch Simon's face; "...always the best," he was sure he heard her say.

Aaron set the food down on the coffee table, turned and pushed his way back into the kitchen. Something in his head was scratching, rustling; interfering with his thoughts and mood. He mustn't stall, he thought. Mustn't lose sight of what he had to do today. She needed to know—there was no way he could allow this to go on; for his sake as well as hers.

He felt oddly displaced when he returned to the front room and had to blink several times in an effort to anchor himself. He marched over to Leanne, gripping her arm and turning her. "We do need that other table," he said. She sipped her wine, gazing at him through intoxicated eyes. "Simon," he said, turning to him. "Would you mind...?"

Simon glanced at Leanne, shrugged. "No problem."

Aaron led him out of the front room and down the hall, the scratching intensifying. They walked past the downstairs bathroom, its door open, their forms passing by in the mirror on the wall. Aaron reached the utilities room, ushered Simon inside. Quietly closed the door behind them both.

The noise in Aaron's head was ferocious now, blocking out all other sound.

Simon turned to him and paled.

"I know what you are," Aaron said, flatly.

Before Simon could reply, Aaron shoved him hard, sending him flying into the wall, sliding down it with blazing eyes. *"...the fuck?"*

Aaron seized the lighter fluid, unscrewed it. Threw the contents over Simon and then spat on him. Simon fought to stand up, but Aaron forced him to the floor with a swift kick and stamp of his foot. Aaron tipped out the remainder of the bottle, then scrambled through his pockets for his lighter.

One flick, two flicks of the wheel, and then there was flame—Simon gasped, fire racing up his arm.

"You *fuck*—" Simon managed, but then his midriff was on fire too and Aaron swung himself around and burst out of the room to evade the flames. Simon charged but Aaron's sleeved hands shoved him again, sending him spiralling into the hall, kicking, writhing and screaming. Then Simon was up onto his feet, scurrying toward the front room, shrieking at the top of his lungs as flames consumed his entire body.

Everyone was screaming now and, as Aaron fell against the wall, he watched their guests dash past, clamouring for the exit. From where he was standing, he could see bright orange serpents writhing all over the curtains in the front room.

Leanne stumbled out into the hall, gasping, sobbing hysterically. He seized her arms, turned her to him. Her eyes were huge and wide, filled with an emotion he had never seen in her before. He could hear a long, agonised wail echoing throughout the house, but didn't bat an eyelid.

"Stay," he shouted. "*I'm* here. There mustn't be anyone... nobody else, Leanne."

She began to squirm and fight, stark terror carved into her features.

He tried to pull her close, but she broke free of him and ran.

"You don't know what it was!" he shrieked after her. "What was hiding!"

She flew out of the door, howling and screaming at the world. He turned and started toward the front room, wanting to see it reveal itself. But something was blocking the passage of his throat, rising swiftly toward his twitching, swelling mouth. He resumed walking, spluttering, coughing and retching. Then, pausing, twisting wildly around, he focused his gaze on his face reflected in the bathroom mirror.

His image gagged as it glared back. Desperately, he wanted to howl, to scream, but he couldn't because his face was convulsing and there was an enormous spider's leg emerging from his open mouth.

Without You I'm Nothing

Wind howled, thunder rolled, rain blinded my eyes. I zipped my coat up, sprinted across the car park and took refuge in the Cheese & Grain. I stood sheltering from the storm in the bustling reception area, eyes glued to the window.

Outside, merchants and traders bundled produce into black bin sacks, dismantled stalls and lifted iron poles into the backs of vans. I listened to the hubbub of the indoor market – people buying, selling, haggling. I smelt slabs of meat sizzling on grills, French cheeses and an assortment of exotic herbs and foreign spices.

Someone tugged at my sleeve. I turned to see a young woman with jade-green eyes smiling at me.

She blushed. "Oh," she said. "You don't recognise me."

"Should I?"

She put a hand over her mouth. "God," she said, "sorry! I thought you were somebody else."

She turned away and I awkwardly stood there watching the rain stream down the windowpane. Then, after a pause, she turned again and said, "You're a Capricorn."

I narrowed my eyes. "Do I *know* you?" She shook her head. "I mean, you thought I was…"

"My mistake. You look nothing like him. Up close, I mean."

"Who did you think I was?"

"A friend."

127

She glanced outside. "Looks like the rain's beginning to ease." She took a deep breath. "I'm Anja. I'm a Gemini. Listen, do you fancy grabbing a coffee?"

She must have seen the look on my face, because she added: "No big deal. Just, I haven't got a lot on and I could do with the company." She smiled again and I knew there was no way I was going to say no.

We sat in *Cordero Lounge* on stools beneath a print of Van Gogh's *The Starry Night*. It turned out Anja lived in Frome. She owned a top-floor flat above a popular Aromatherapy shop. She was in her second year of an Open University degree in Psychology and was hoping to become an educational psychologist by the end of it.

"I'm fascinated by people," she said. "By behaviour, mainly. I want to know how we work. What makes us tick, you know?" She flicked her hair away from her eyes. "What do you do?"

"I'm an IS engineer. I travel around a lot, fixing computers, installing software, that kind of thing."

She nodded. "You enjoy it?"

"Not really. Sometimes I feel like I'm in this rut, you know? Driving out to the same old places, fixing the same computers..."

She laughed. "The moon enters Capricorn on Friday so the time is ripe for change. The full moon at the end of the month signifies an emotional high tide. It's the best time to make changes, you know."

"You really believe in that stuff?"

"I'm *intrigued*, I guess. Over the years I've studied astrology, cosmology, palmistry..."

"You read palms?"

"Occasionally," she replied.

"Think you could read mine?" I stuck my hand out. "I've always wanted my palm read."

She leaned over the table and I caught the scent of her perfume. It smelt oddly familiar somehow. She took hold of my hand and said, "You have two brothers and one sister. Your father passed away just over a year ago."

I stared at her. "You got that from looking at my palm?"

She nodded and smiled.

That smile was bewitching.

We went back to her flat. It was small, much like my own. The single window in the sitting room had the most astonishing view over Frome. She'd replaced all the doors with bead curtains, strung up fairy lights and painted the walls a lurid shade of crimson.

"What's that?" I asked, pointing to a strange prickly plant and a blackened crystal on a fold-out table.

"Some of my occult stuff," she said.

We sat together on her sofa and talked for ages. She said all the right things, seemed to know so much about me. Later, after sharing a bottle of wine, we made love in her bed. In the darkness she moaned and writhed, her fingers splayed out across my chest, her green eyes shining.

That night I had this disturbing dream. I was alone in Anja's flat. On the mantelpiece, candle flames fluttered like tongues. I drifted toward the mirror and there, hanging in the darkness, was my own blood-red reflection. My image quickly faded and then Anja appeared, green eyes burning, her hands shooting out and shattering glass, pulling me through the frame into a dark abyss.

***

"Don't go," she said as I dressed for work the next morning.

"What do you mean 'don't go?'" I searched amongst our clothes on the carpet for my jacket. "I *have* to go."

She stretched herself out across the bed. "Stay. Phone in sick or something."

I stared at her.

She stared right back with those cold green eyes.

I said, "Why don't we go out tonight? My treat. I'll take you to that Italian on Vicarage Street."

"Sounds nice," she said as I pulled my car keys out of my pocket. "But why can't we stay here? Just you and me, Chris. Wouldn't it be great if we never had to leave this flat again?"

She sat up, wrapping her arms around herself. "Sorry," she whispered. "I know some of the things I say are strange. I get carried away, that's all. I don't know why I just said that, about never leaving the flat." She sighed and hung her head. "You must think me weird."

"No," I said, shrugging into my jacket, but her glassy stare remained fixed to the duvet and she said nothing more.

130

***

It was a week later. Anya and I had arranged to meet at my place for seven. I left work early and was back in Frome by six. Rain scratched at discs of light around streetlamps. I grabbed some groceries in the Co-Op and a cheap bottle of Pinot Noir. Then, just as I was leaving, I saw Helen standing under the awning outside Iceland.

Helen's a work colleague. She's tall and thin and has long brown hair and a bright, pretty smile. "What are you doing here?" I asked, crossing the road to meet her. "Thought you'd moved to Wells?"

"I did," she said, smoothing her hair out of her eyes, "but my mother lives in Frome. I was off today so I thought I'd do some shopping for her."

I told her about what had gone on at work today and about the team meeting we'd scheduled for Monday. "Fancy grabbing a coffee?" I said.

"Sure," she replied. "Why not?"

We took a table in *Cordero Lounge*. We talked work for a while, then about life in general.

"Feels like my life's gone off on one," I said as I stared into my coffee. "I had all these set goals and plans. I wanted to be married by the time I was thirty. Have kids and everything." I looked up, gazing at the swirling brushstrokes in the Van Gogh print on the wall. "Is that sad?"

She shook her head. "No, not sad. It'll happen, Chris." She chewed her lip. "You seeing anyone at the moment?"

"Yeah. Well, kind of. It's a bit…strange, to be honest."

131

"Strange?"

I laughed. "Yeah. The things she knows about me. There's definitely a spark, a connection, but it sort of feels contrived. I don't know how to explain it…"

She traced her finger around the rim of her coffee mug. "Is this the person you spoke about before?"

I shook my head, momentarily confused. "I don't think so."

"Me and my bloke, Tom," she said, "have been on and off for years. It's just, we get ideals in our head, don't we. Of how relationships should be. Perhaps we should just face up to the fact that we can never find the perfect person. It's an impossible…"

She stopped midsentence. Her eyes locked on something outside. I turned quickly. "What?" I said, looking through the window.

The street was deserted.

"There was a woman out there just now," she said, "staring in at us."

"Where did she go?"

"Not sure."

"Listen," I said, reaching for my wallet, "I'd better go." I smiled. "I really enjoyed our chat."

"Me too." Helen grinned. "We'll have to do it again some time."

I hurried home, oblivious to the low rumbles of thunder coming from above. Rain tore through trees, created hypnotic patterns in puddles. I turned down the narrow lane at the back of the garages and saw Anja in the communal garden outside the flats.

"Anja?"

We stood staring at each other for a moment. Then she lowered her eyes and said, "Are you going to let me in or what?"

I let her in, then closed the door behind us. Anja perched herself on the foot of the bed. "What's the matter?" I asked.

"Who was that girl you were talking to?"

"Girl?"

"You know, the brunette. I saw you in the café together."

"So?" I stared incredulously at her. "Her name's Helen. We work together; she's in town visiting her mum. Look, what's this about?"

"What were you talking about?"

I ignored her and walked off into the kitchen. Opened a bottle of wine and poured myself a glass. I heard her feet pad into the room and then turned, struggling to hide my anger.

"The first time we met," she said. "In the Cheese & Grain. Then, later, in the café. What would you have liked to have heard? How could I *really* have impressed you?"

I didn't respond, alarm bells ringing inside my head.

She drew a hand across her eyes. "I've fucked up again, haven't I." Her voice trembled. "I can't help how I am. I mean, nobody could love you like I do. And you don't ever seem to understand. Without you, Chris, I'm nothing."

I stared at her. "But we've only known each other for a week."

She hung her head and laughed bitterly at the floor. "Next time," she said. "Next time I *promise* I'll get it right."

I had another lucid dream that night. Anja was leaning over me, whispering words I just didn't understand. I smelt something burning deep inside the room. She straightened up as I tried to focus on her voice, to hear her words, an enigmatic smile creeping across her face.

"Don't hate me," she said. "It's a chance to start afresh. The onus is on me, right? To make it good. To get it *perfect*."

I stared at the blackened crystal in her hand. She touched me on the face with trembling fingers and then there…*is*…a flash, and I…I don't remember… I don't remember anything else.

I look around, confused. Dawn light steals through the curtains. I'm disorientated, feel vaguely nauseated. I can't even remember what day of the week it is. I fling back the duvet and pull on some clothes, drifting over to the gilt-framed mirror by the door. My face stares back, so pale and blank looking.

Outside, dead leaves swirl across pavements. I slip in and out of shops in a daze. Clouds stack over trees and chimney pots. Then a sudden downpour streaks my face and I zip my coat up and dash for shelter in the Cheese & Grain.

Inside I listen to the rain chatter on slate tiles, slosh through broken guttering, whisper against grimy windows. I hear the bustle of the indoor market, watch the rain outside make hypnotic circles in wide, dark puddles.

Someone tugs at my sleeve.

I turn and see a face that is, for a split-second, strikingly familiar.

The young woman retracts her hand. "Sorry," she says, putting that hand over her mouth. "My mistake." Then she takes her hand away again and says, softly, "I thought you were somebody else."

Horror's Heart

Kincaid stared up at the decaying apartment complex, a mixture of dread, fear and something vaguely like hope coursing through his veins. *What I'd give to just slip into a state of emotional numbness,* he thought. He was so tired of feeling. Tired of this world and of himself, too.

He clenched and unclenched his hands. Pushed through the main communal door and entered the building.

Rubble, twisted pieces of metal and broken glass lay scattered across the floor. He edged around the debris, taking and climbing the stairs, wood clattering together in his backpack. He thought of the creature he was about to meet – the heart of the horror which had terrorised this city. How she might offer an alternative form of existence. Help him to forget the family he'd had. The crippling self-loathing that never went away…

He reached the top floor, gripped the handrail and paused momentarily for breath. A haunting piano riff playing alongside some achingly sad violins was coming from a room just along the corridor.

The door to that apartment stood ajar. Kincaid opened it wide, scanning the curios, ornaments and trinkets on display. An animal skull with twisting antlers. An abstract painting depicting two black holes leaking crimson paint. A goldfish bowl with a human skull inside. A large coffin, the lid raised, its interior lined with velvet.

The music was coming from an old-fashioned gramophone, its strange, repetitive melody echoing around and around inside his head. It had done its job of bringing him here, of leading him to her lair.

Stood at the window was the creature he was seeking, a tall and slender figure, completely unclothed and as pale as marble.

She glanced at him as he entered the room. "I was wondering when you were going to come."

Kincaid froze, his stony silence prompting her to turn around completely. His heart trembled. She was beautiful. Monstrous, too.

"I've been listening to all the shouting and cheering," she said. "Watching the marches and pyres being built. You've won, right? Just me left now." She tilted her head to one side. "You don't look capable of killing to me. How many have you slain, then?"

It took him a moment to find his voice. "Hundreds. Over a thousand, maybe."

She brushed back the midnight stream of her hair with both hands. "I'm their leader," she said, "and you've found me. You must be feeling pretty pleased with yourself."

"Doesn't the sun…?" He waved vaguely in the direction of the window.

She laughed and shook her head. "I won't go away. *Can't* go away. I am infinite. I am eternal."

He slid the backpack off his shoulder and put it down on the surface of the floor. "I've killed," he said, "just so I can get close to you. I want you all to myself." A smile tugged at his lips. "The Agency sent for me because I'm the best. Although I'm nothing like them. I'm as much an outsider as you are."

"Shouldn't you at least be wielding one of those right now?" She nodded at the pack between his feet.

"I hate what I am," he said, ignoring the question. "Detest what I'm a part of. Feelings are such awful, shackling things."

"Pass me a stake," she said, sounding bored already.

Kincaid shrugged and then unzipped his backpack. He pulled out a stake, straightened it and handed it to her. She gripped it in a chalk-white fist. Held it close to her breast, pressing the sharpened point to her heart. Her other hand grabbed it, too. Before he could say or do anything, she stabbed herself, thrusting the stake hard and deep into her chest, her face convulsing in a series of violent spasms.

He jolted forward, hands reaching out for nothing. Then her features relaxed. Her arms collapsed to her sides.

"Told you," she said. "Nothing can make me go away."

Her hands were on the stake again. He watched in disbelief as she slid it back out. It dropped and clattered to the floor.

Kincaid closed his eyes.

"I've wanted you for such a long time," he said. "Since it all began to fall apart. I don't care about any of it. My life. Them out there. Only you. I only ever think about you now."

The music stopped, the gramophone clicking still.

His eyelids lifted.

She was reaching for him with open arms.

He shuffled toward her, those arms snaking around his neck, her teeth swiftly finding the pulse point in his throat. A flash of pain – and then he was fading away from himself, throwing off the shackles, passing from one plane of existence to another.

The next thing he knew, he was sat propped upright on a chair. He lifted his head, noticing she'd drawn the curtains to block out the sunlight.

She was standing over him, grinning, her eyes big, black and wide.

He put his hand to his neck. Winced and then brought it away again. Blood glistened on his fingertips.

"We needn't be alone anymore," she whispered. "I'm the monster of your world, you're the horror of mine." She offered him her hand. "We were made for each other."

He gripped her fingers, rising to his full height. They made their way over to her bed. She laid inside it first, arms reaching for him again. He gazed down at her ashen face, her smile, those abyssal eyes…

"Now, it starts over," she said. "We begin again."

He lowered himself into her embrace, her arms and legs wrapping around him, her mouth fastening on to his throat.

They might unleash a second plague, he thought. Become king and queen of some twisted, necrotic empire.

How do I feel, he wondered?

She reached up, grabbing hold of an ornate handle and pulling the coffin lid down on them both. Nothing, he realised, devoured by darkness.

Finally, I feel nothing.

Bequeathed

Way before the sickness, way before the decline and transformation, I visited a nondescript council house on St. John's Road, opposite the flats where the Ragman lived.

It was a brittle, bright October morning. I drifted to the door and knocked twice on its frosted pane of glass. A curtain twitched so I knew somebody was home.

The door jolted open, an elderly man peering out at me. His back was hunched, his hair white, his fingers long and bent and twisted by arthritis. "Mr Benedict?" I asked and he nodded. "Got your message. I'm your local Police Community Support Officer."

He glanced over my shoulder at some indeterminable spot behind me, then ushered me inside, closing the door behind us.

The front room was small and cramped and smelled of cigarettes, damp and furniture polish. It was furnished with a couple of uncomfortable looking armchairs, a longcase clock, a coffee table and a stained, hard knotted rug.

He gestured for me to sit with a flick of his fingers. "Cup of tea?"

"No," I said, "thanks."

He eased himself into the chair opposite mine. "Thank you for coming. It's actually quite nice to have company for a change." He looked up at the window. "Oh," he said, rising, beckoning me, "let me show you what the problem is."

141

I found my feet, watching him pull the curtains back to reveal the flats opposite. "There's something going on over there," he said. "Kids coming and going all hours of day and night. Not just kids sometimes. They knock on the window to a flat, wanting to be let in."

"Think it's drug related?"

He shrugged and snatched the curtains shut again.

"I'll keep an eye on it," I said. "If you recognise anyone going in, pass me their names. Also, any vehicles you see outside the address; try and get their indexes. I'll give you my mobile number and email address before I go."

There was a framed photograph standing on the windowsill, worn and faded, but I discerned a woman with long grey hair and a bright, pretty smile. "Your wife?" I asked, nodding at it.

"Aye," he said and sighed. "She died last year."

"Oh. Sorry to hear that."

"After she died, I didn't think I could cope with being alone." He knuckled his left eye. "They say time heals. Well, things haven't got any better for me, that's for sure."

Back at the station I told Clare, my beat manager, about the flat.

"Check Quickaddress out for a name, see if they're known to us," she said, grabbing her hat and radio. "Got to dash – Shopwatch meeting in half an hour. Sounds like you got some good intel there, Keith."

She paused, picking a loose strand of hair away from her eyes. "I was on your patch the other day.

142

St. John's Road, Armstrong Road, St. Mary's Road." She fastened her radio to the front of her body armour. "The residents there seem *defeated*. The gardens are a mess, there's junk heaped up in the streets. It feels like people are giving up, you know?"

I nodded. "But what can we do? I've been talking to the council and some local businesses about funding a youth club or internet café, but no one's willing to stump up the cash."

"Drugs are an easy escape." She snatched up a set of keys from off her desk. "Might be worth visiting the flat yourself – see who's there, scope it out a bit."

"Think I will."

"Good luck," she said, and left.

Terri was watching TV when I got home. I kicked off my boots and entered the lounge.

"What's this crap?" I asked, nodding at the unconvincing actress crying onscreen.

Terri didn't reply.

I walked into the kitchen and grabbed myself a beer. "Remember they've got to last you all week," she shouted.

"Whatever," I mumbled back.

The credits were rolling when I returned and Terri was sat forward in her chair, her eyes red-rimmed and puffy. "What's up?"

She stared at her hands. "Tired, that's all."

We were quiet for a moment. I perched myself on the edge of the armchair, watching names scroll down the TV screen. "How's Joseph?"

"Asleep."

"Aren't you going to wake him? I mean, he won't sleep tonight if he…"

"What do you care?" she snapped, turning on me. "I'm the one who gets up, remember?"

I closed my eyes, concentrating on the sound of the traffic outside.

"How's work?" she asked at last.

I opened my eyes and glared at her. "I don't want to worry you with it. You've got enough to worry about, looking after Joseph all day." *You're always tired,* I thought with a stab of resentment, getting up, walking out of the room and leaving her to her soaps.

Joseph was sound asleep in the nursery, his tiny fists clenched tight, his eyelids twitching. I stroked his face, trying to feel something.

"Gorgeous, isn't he?" Terri whispered and I turned to see her in the doorway, leant against its unvarnished frame, her arms folded across her chest.

"Yes," I said and fixed a smile in place.

She walked to the cot and drew the blanket up around his shoulders. I stood there watching, guilt stealing over me. "It was something Clare said," I blurted as she straightened, her long hair sliding across her face.

"Sorry?"

"Clare. From work." I cringed at the slight tremor I heard in my own voice. "We were talking about my beat. She said the people living on St. John's Road, Armstrong Road, St. Mary's Road…they all seem *defeated.* There's a resignation

144

about them…people don't seem to care about anything anymore. Made me feel like shit, as if I'm not doing enough."

"Oh, Keith." She touched my face. "We've talked about this before. You're perfectly suited to that role because you *care*." Her hand dropped away and she smiled.

Later, while she was showering, I called Kate on my mobile. She answered almost immediately. "My sister's round in a minute. I'm busy. What…?"

"Can I see you tomorrow?" I interrupted, glancing nervously around at the door.

Kate's twenty-one and lives on her own in St. Mary's Road. She had a problem with kids kicking footballs against her window and we got chatting and hit it off…in more ways than one.

"Don't know," she said. "I've got to take Mum to her hospital appointment."

"What time?" The shower stopped. I heard Terri pull back the shower curtain.

"Three o'clock."

"I'm on an early. I could pop in during the morning."

A pause. Then, when she answered, I could almost picture the smile on her thin, painted lips. "You be in uniform?"

"Of course."

Terri opened the bathroom door.

"Gotta go," I said, killing the call. Then I smiled and got up and fetched myself another beer.

"I'm moving to Birmingham."

145

Kate's flat was poky and dimly-lit. On the sofa, my radio crackled; a road traffic collision involving a car and a push bike. It wasn't anywhere near the St. John's estate, so I didn't have to worry about it.

Our clothes lay strewn around us on the floor. "You're not coming back?" I asked, sitting up on one elbow, my voice small and brittle sounding.

Kate flashed me a smile. "I'm making a go of things with Seb."

"Why?"

"Because I love him."

I laughed. "But you've been sleeping with me."

"And it's been good," she said, stroking the knuckles of my hand, "right? But we both knew it wouldn't be permanent."

I lay my head in her lap. "I'll miss you," I said, after a pause.

She stared at me and at last I met her eyes, trying, and failing, to read what they were conveying.

Kate was silent as she watched me get dressed. The radio crackled – the controller directing a unit to an incident in Shepton Mallet. I wasn't even listening. "If you aren't happy you should leave her," Kate said, pulling on her bathrobe.

"Who says I'm not happy?"

"Oh, Keith."

"Good luck," I said, shrugging into my body armour and making for the door.

I walked down St. Mary's Road, throwing one last look over my shoulder. She was staring out of her window, her expression one of discernible relief.

I kept on walking until I reached the top of St. John's Road. Broken fence panels shivered in the wind. I made my way over to the flats, seeing Mr Benedict – pale, gaunt, unshaven – at his front window. I waved to him but he didn't wave back.

I turned to the flats and pushed at the door, discovering it unlocked. The communal hall stank strongly of piss. I closed the door behind me and turned to the flat on my left.

The door to the property stood ajar, its handle hanging lower than it should and sagging. I peered in and saw two youths talking to somebody just out of my line of sight. One kid had short dark hair and a pimpled face, a leather coat draped over his shoulder. "I know you're not asleep," he hissed. "*Look* at me!" He stormed across the room, disappearing from sight.

The other youth – dressed in a combat jacket and black *Cradle of Filth* T-shirt – looked up and around, the colour draining from off his face. "Shit," he said, and the door was suddenly snatched open, the first youth reappearing before me. "Oh," he said. "Hi."

"What's going on?" I asked.

"Just leaving," the youth muttered as he brushed past me, pushing out of the main door and exiting the flats. The other youth followed, glancing sheepishly at me as he left.

I turned my attention to the flat, to the open door and poked my head inside. "Hullo?"

The flat was unpainted, dirty and the stench of what might have been rotten fruit carried in the air. There were hardly any furnishings – just an

147

armchair pushed up against a wall in the corner. Slumped in it was an elderly man, his head lowered, his grubby hands clasped together in his lap. I couldn't see his face because his hair was in the way, but he was dressed in a filthy suit, shirt and waistcoat. Coarse, wheezing sounds bubbled in his throat.

For a moment I feared he was hurt; that I'd stumbled upon the scene of an assault, or worse.

"You okay?" I asked, standing over him. The male raised his head and I gasped. His face was covered in growths, pustules and sores. Black pus dribbled down the side of his misshapen nose from an ugly weal on his forehead. One of his eyes was swollen shut, his lips split and moving wordlessly within a fiercely tangled beard.

He leaned forward, trying to touch me.

I instinctively stepped back.

He moaned as if he were trying to speak, to communicate, but I couldn't make out the words.

I gripped my radio, finger poised over the transmission button. My first thought was that he'd been beaten, that he was in need of emergency assistance. Then I realised those welts couldn't possibly have come from a beating… This was a medical affliction, signs of some horrible, debilitating disease. "Do you need help?" I said, crouching, feeling my face twist involuntarily into a mask of disgust.

He shook his head, his one good eye staring at the floor.

"Do you live here?" I asked, as loud and as clear as I could.

He nodded.

"Who were those kids?"

No reply.

"You should keep your door closed," I said, straightening, standing over him again. "Get the lock fixed."

I lingered there for just a moment longer, wondering if I should do anything more. "You sure you're all right?"

"Leeth *melone,*" he rasped, suddenly.

My shoulders sagged and I nodded at him, turned and left.

Terri was busy cooking Bolognese when I got in. She was wearing a short black dress with a ribbed low-cut top. "How was your day?" she asked as I stepped into the kitchen.

"Not bad." I peeled off my coat. "Where's Joseph?"

"Mum's." Her smile was tentative, barely a flicker. "Thought we could do with a night in on our own. Some quality *us* time, eh?" She gestured to the lounge with a nod of her head. "Sit down, dinner's almost ready. I'll bring it in in a sec."

We ate in front of the TV. Nothing much was on and I kept tuning into the sound of the rain as it scratched against the window. Once we'd eaten, I put our plates on the coffee table and turned to her.

A bittersweet smile spread across her face. "Sorry," she said.

"What for?"

"Yesterday. I was in a right old mood."

"It's all right."

"No. No it's not all right."

My gaze drifted back to the TV.

"I've had a really nice day," she said, stretching her legs out. "I've had my nails done and I bought myself a brand-new blouse from M&S. Caught up with Heather, too." Heather was Terri's sister.

She moved in close, smiling, but I pulled away before she could kiss me. "Sorry," I said, "I'm tired. It's been a long day."

She sat back, stung. "Oh," she said, crossing her arms across her chest. "We never want it at the same time, do we. Maybe…" She tailed off.

She laid her head against me, then wrapped her arm around my waist. Moments later she was asleep.

I wanted to tell her everything then. Wanted to wake her up and make things right. Instead, I placed a hand over my face and sobbed quietly, ever-so-softly through my fingers.

Terri never stirred, never heard a thing.

The morning was cold and dark, rags of cloud drifting across the leaden sky. The rain held off until I reached St. John's Road, where Mr Benedict was tending to his garden. He'd cut back the grass, weeds and nettles and hung up a flower basket in his front porch. "Someone's been busy," I said over the hedge.

He looked up, a pair of secateurs in his hands. "Been meaning to do this for ages. Didn't have it in me before."

"You're looking well."

"Aye," he said. "Can't complain."

I nodded at the flats opposite. "Any more activity?"

His cheeks reddened and he pinched his nose. "Pretty sure there's nothing going on. Probably was reading too much into it."

Mr Benedict began snipping at his rose bush. "They're local residents," he said. "Good Samaritans, making sure he's okay."

"You've seen him?"

"Aye," he said, and I fancied for a moment he was vaguely irritated by me. "Visited him yesterday as a matter of fact." He rubbed the back of his hand in his cardigan. "Went round with the neighbours. As I said, it's all in order." He shrugged. "Sorry I wasted your time."

Just as he finished speaking, four lads in hoodies stepped out of the flats. I looked up, listening in on their conversation.

"He's fucked," said one.

"What do we care?" said another. "As long as he sorts us out."

"What if he...?" began a third, then they noticed me, their eyes narrowing, their elbows nudging one another. Then they turned and walked off at speed, heading down St. John's Road. The first drop of rain struck my cheek as I spun, Mr Benedict, secateurs still in hand, watching me run.

I jogged past the vandalised telephone kiosk on the corner of Armstrong Road, the Residents Centre, chip shop and the convenience store. Finally I reached Rodden Road, seeing the youths duck beneath the old railway bridge. I quickened my pace, but by the time I reached the bridge they were

151

nowhere to be seen. They must have scrambled up the embankment onto the tracks, I thought and turned back the way I had come. Then a figure emerged from the bushes beside the bridge and I recognised him instantly as the kid in the combat jacket and *Cradle of Filth* T-shirt from yesterday.

He stared at me, the wind driving his hair into his dead white face.

"Where are the others?" I asked.

"Gone home." He pulled in a breath. "I thought, perhaps, if I talked to you…"

"What's going on with that guy in the flat?"

His whole face was twitching, as though the flesh were trying to tear itself free of the skull. "D-don't take him away. What he can do…well, it's a miracle." The boy rubbed his nose, glancing nervously about us at the rain-lashed street. "People call him the Ragman. We *need* him – this *neighbourhood* needs him." He stepped away from me. "I-I shouldn't have… The others warned me…"

"Wait," I said, but he was off, running flat out, darting up Rodden Road toward St. John's. I let him go, knowing I would never catch him.

I was still thinking about the incident later that night, lying in bed next to Terri. I couldn't for the life of me sleep; too much was going on in my brain for me to switch off. I gave up eventually and carefully climbed out of bed. A part of me wanted to wake Terri and tell her *everything,* but I now sensed there was an easier way of shedding the guilt. I wanted to cast off my disappointment over Kate going, too.

152

Despite the hour I left home and wandered the streets, ending up in the middle of the St. John's estate. I knew I wouldn't be able to resist coming here; it was the ideal time for me to see him. Broken windows emitted drunken voices and the strong reek of cannabis. Dog shit made a minefield of the pavement.

I reached the flats at last, pushing through the unlocked main door. The communal hall was dark and still smelt of urine. I closed the door behind me, then turned to the flat on my left. The broken door widened as I shoved against it, stale, dust-choked darkness enveloping me.

I immediately discerned a familiar shape in the corner, seated in his armchair, and as I walked over to him, my nose wrinkled in disgust. "I understand you can help," I said, crouching, trying not to breathe in that sickening smell of decay.

His head jerked to one side and a guttural moan escaped him. A cloud of flies shifted across his face. Then he reached out a hand and I nodded, smiled, and felt his fingers grip my shoulder. His good eye opened, glittering wetly in the dark. "Puh-puh-*puhleease,* g-g-god."

"Can you help me?" I asked, trying hard not to sound desperate. Then his eye began to cloud, to glaze over, his voice dropping to a whisper. *"At lassssst,"* he said, and he released his grip.

Something was wrong.

I got to my feet, my head flashing with strange lights and colours. I felt weirdly nauseous and afraid. I reached out, grabbing his waistcoat, shaking him hard.

No response.

"Fuck," I whispered.

I let go, glancing round at the door.

Phone someone. Get help.

Instead, I ran out the door and fled into night's uncaring arms.

Terri said, "Don't worry about it."

It was two weeks later. She was leant against the bathroom door as I was staring into the mirror at the sores that had appeared on my forehead, nose and neck. I touched them with trembling fingers before dropping my hand to my side and grimacing. One of them had split, oozing black pus.

She drifted toward me. Outside, rain hissed against the mottled windowpane and I thought I could hear thunder. She was naked, her hair hanging in her face. "Oh, that was *good,*" she smiled, her eyes shining behind her hair. "Can we do it again later?"

She reached out, stroking my arm. "You won't want me soon," I said, my gaze still glued to my image.

"Don't say that! *Course* I'll want you."

From the next room, Joseph began to cry.

"Uh-oh," she said.

"I'll go."

I rocked Joseph back off to sleep in my arms. I stared out the window, seeing only a dismal grey wall of rain. Once Joseph had settled, I lowered him into the cot and tugged his blanket over him. I touched his face with blistered fingers, then returned to our bedroom and Terri.

154

I got into bed. "Is he all right?" she asked.

"Fine."

"Hold me," she said, and I rolled over and held her.

Later, in the middle of the night, I woke with a start.

"What's wrong?" Terri asked, sitting up, throwing back our duvet and reaching for me.

"I can't see," I shrieked, clasping a hand over my eye. "I can't *see!*"

I ran into the bathroom, squinting, trying to see my disfigured reflection in the mirror above the sink.

The skin around the left eye was puckered and swollen, the eyelid seemingly unable to lift. My skin was a shrivelled mess of fresh pustules, blisters and sores.

Terri flung her arms around me and told me everything was going to be all right, but I knew it wouldn't. Not now.

Not ever.

It's Friday night and I'm upstairs all alone in the bedroom. The curtains are drawn, the light switched off. I'm sitting on the edge of the bed, absently listening to the noises of the street. I've hung a white sheet over the mirror so I don't have to look at myself. I've been off work for three weeks and have resigned myself to the fact that I won't be going back.

I feel bone weary and can barely eat or speak now. I just sit and stare at the wall, or at the faded floral pattern on the curtains, or at the strange growths on the backs of my hands. The stench of rotten fruit perpetually clings to me.

I hear the front door open, Terri and her sister Heather talking in hushed tones down in the hall. Heather lost her job last week and her husband's been diagnosed with prostate cancer. Terri told me she's in a bad place, which almost made me want to laugh out loud.

I can hear them mounting the stairs, Heather whispering something, Terri replying that it's going to be all right, that I can help, that I can siphon the pain and make everything better...

The bedroom door creaks open, Heather letting out a small, startled cry. I try to form a smile, but my mouth hurts and my lips split and weep a little.

Terri comes sweeping over, running her hand through my hair, kissing me and saying, "Oh, my love, my love."

With one watery eye I gaze at Heather, who looks upon me in horror. She turns to Terri and asks, "What do I do?"

Terri grins. "Go to him."

"Keith?" Heather whispers and I try to smile again, to speak, but the noise which leaves me is guttural and wrong. I hold out my arms in an automated fashion. Heather collapses into them, gasping, tears running down the length of her face and as I pull her in tight, I hope and pray to god to die.

Made Of Stone

Chapter 1

"I baked a chocolate cake this morning," Sadie told the headstone, trying her best to smile. "We probably won't get round to eating it. I only baked it because it reminded me of you." Her smile vanished. "I know how much you used to love your chocolate cake. How you used to end up with it all round your mouth. It used to make us laugh so hard."

My gaze fixed itself to the ground.

There was only so much of this I could take.

Sadie would often express her frustration that I wouldn't talk. But we weren't really talking to Archie, were we.

The trees quietly rustled around us. The temperature was dropping. I couldn't interrupt her, not while she had more to say.

"I'm painting all the time," she said. "Usually portraits of you, my darling. Trying to imagine what you might have looked like now, based on the photographs and memories I have."

I didn't like looking at the photographs. Sadie could study them for hours. Sometimes I would have to come downstairs in the middle of the night and make her pack them all away.

"Well," trying to force another smile, "I suppose we'd better go." She nodded toward our house. "We're only over there, remember? And I carry you around with me everywhere. A part of you is with me now," she clasped a hand to her chest, "here; inside. And a part of me is with you, too." She pulled in a breath. "Wherever you are."

***

Later that evening, I noticed Sadie was reading a worn, dogeared copy of *Frankenstein*.

She saw me looking.

"Did you know," she said, "that Mary Shelley had five pregnancies but only one surviving child?"

"It was common for children to die young those days."

"Her first child," Sadie said, undeterred by my air of general disinterest, "was a little girl named Clara. She died when she was just eight days old. Shelley wrote about a dream she had, where her child came back to life. It had only been cold, she wrote, and that when she rubbed it by the fire, it had lived again."

I closed my eyes. "Why don't you try and sleep?"

She sighed, then rolled away from me and switched off the lamp.

"There's so much pain in the world," she whispered at the darkness. "So much unavoidable, inescapable pain. No wonder people change, Nick. No wonder they become all twisted and bent out of shape. They don't mean to. It's just the pain and the hurt that turns them into monsters."

Chapter 2

"So," Lucy asked me, a couple of days later. "When are you going to tell her?"

We were sat together in Lucy's flat. As I contemplated a reply, I surveyed our surroundings. Lucy was an amateur photographer. There were photos pegged to lines stretching across the length of the room. She took lots of pictures of places around town and the way she caught them made them seem different and otherworldly. Maybe it was the camera she used, or the effect of the lighting perhaps. But she could make me see aspects of our town in new and arresting ways.

She laid her hand on my knee, giving it a squeeze. Her other hand drew her hair back away from her eyes. "It's plainly clear that you're only with her now out of sympathy," she said. "It's like you feel you're under some obligation, or duty, to stay. But the longer you leave it, the worse it's going to be."

I glanced at her again, remembering how she'd told me once that she loved me.

I saw her as a chance to begin again.

To become someone new.

She clasped her hands together, pushed them between her thighs. "You don't want to feel trapped like this. You know it's not right. You have to look after yourself. Put yourself first, Nick. Put *us* first. And if she was being honest with herself, she'd accept it's over, too."

My gaze fixed on the many pictures on the wall of Lucy and I smiling and cosying up together. Looking happy. Content. That felt so unreal. Everywhere I looked, there was us in small square windows, frozen blissfully in time.

She saw me looking. "In this flat," she whispered, "between these walls, my world is all about you. But out there," she nodded toward the window, "we're separate. And I want the two to meet, Nick. I want that *so* much." Another sad smile. "I want to walk out there with you, my head held high. Not to be sneaking around behind people's backs like this. It's not fair on me. Not fair on her, either, really."

160

Chapter 3

The day I left Sadie will always stay with me; there are moments that will be painfully etched on my memory forever. I remember seeing Lucy first. It had been raining and she refused to let me enter her flat.

"I'm not going to wait for you forever," she said, leaning against the doorframe, watching me get colder and wetter out on the street. "I have a life too. The clock's ticking mister. I'm not getting any younger."

"Lucy… *Please*. Just let me come in. We can talk about it inside. Not out here in the street."

"Not until you give me an answer." She folded her arms across her chest. "I've been waiting and waiting. Carrying on but there's still no end in sight. What's it going to be, eh? Me or her?"

"I'll tell her," I said, nodding my head.

"Now?" she asked. "Will you tell her now?"

"Now."

And so that was exactly what happened; Lucy drove me to the house and I went in there and told Sadie everything.

It passed by in a blur. I've managed to successfully blank out most of the details. But I do remember the look in Sadie's eyes. The terrible, awful hurt.

I'd seen it before.

After Archie.

After everything we went through together.

I felt Archie's presence so keenly it was difficult to speak. But I remained hard, cold and resolute.

And then I was gone, filled with so much shame and regret and much relief, too.

Lucy was waiting for me in her car.

I put my small bag of packed belongings in the footwell. Sat in the car beside her and closed the door.

She looked at me with her big, dark eyes.

"It's done," I said, and she smiled without saying a single word.

Chapter 4

Ironically, things never worked out between me and Lucy. She helped me to slip away, though, changing the direction my life was heading, but we quickly discovered that we didn't belong together.

I haven't seen her for months now. Think she might have even skipped town.

But I have been thinking lots about Sadie. I need to know she's okay. That she's surviving and she's well. I don't even know for sure that she's still living in our old house, the one behind the cemetery.

I pass through the district where I used to live. An air of neglect has crept in. There are weeds and brambles everywhere. The streets seem so quiet. So still.

I make my way over to my old front door. Maybe she has someone new, I think. I genuinely hope so. I hope she's not alone. I draw in a breath, then knock. No reply. The door's ajar though, and I open it, slowly.

"Sadie?"

This place feels as cold and as still as a mausoleum. I slip inside, staring at all her pictures covering the walls. They appear to fill every patch of wall space – paintings of the house, the garden, us.

Always us.

Together.

As one.

I reach out, touching the three of us, briefly, hesitantly.

One painting depicts Archie as a handsome young man.

I know it's supposed to be him.

He has my colour eyes.

Her hair.

She is standing with him, arms wrapped around his waist. Her hair strangely raised and waving. Words in a balloon coming from her open mouth: *You are in my stone-cold heart.*

"Sadie?" I try again.

Just silence.

I head for the back door.

I think I know where she might be. Where she would go if she wasn't here.

The trees shake their bony fists at the heavens. Dead leaves swirl about my feet.

I see her up ahead, knelt on the earth in front of his headstone.

Of course she would be there. She is wearing her winter coat, I see, the hood pulled up. Surrounding us, black, hollow pairs of eyes catch my wandering gaze. The statues have built up and they appear so lonely, lost and sad. A sea of memorial statues, facing vacantly toward Sadie.

I stop behind her, steeling myself to speak.

"Hi."

She tilts her head just a fraction.

I still cannot see her face. In my head, I'm busy working out how long it's been. What, two years since I last saw her? Three?

"I knew you'd come back," she whispers.

"I came to see how you are," I say. "I needed to know you were okay. I'm sorry I…" I trail off.

The only sound for a moment is the dry rustling of the trees.

"*Here* is where we should be," she replies. "The three of us. Together. You can never imagine how badly I wanted that, Nick." A short pause. "Still do, in fact."

"I wanted it too," I say, but my voice sounds so small and faint, muffled by the rustling I can hear. "But after everything we…"

"You don't know what you did," she says, straightening slowly.

I know now that I shouldn't have come. This is all just a bad mistake.

"Sadie…" I begin.

She starts turning her body toward me.

And I realise the rustling I hear isn't coming from the trees at all.

Carefully, she pulls back the hood of her coat.

The terrible hurt in her eyes has transformed into something else.

Something impossible.

"You want to see how I am?" she asks, the rustling and hissing and slithering amplifying in my ears.

Her wide eyes glow and I realise I won't be leaving this place ever again.

"Well," she says. "Look at me now."

We All Feel Better In The Dark

Craig saw the For-Sale sign standing in the weed-strewn front garden of his parents' house. Once he was baptised, the hope and dream was for them all to live together in his grandfather's place. Grandad had been talking about starting and growing a church for years. Family values carefully shaped and distorted into an uncompromising new religion.

Craig knew he was next in line. Due his initiation tomorrow, in fact. But he had special plans of his own and he fully intended on actioning them first.

He crossed the garden to the front door, clutching a large bunch of pink lilies. He knocked and Mum opened up with a confused expression on her face. "Craig! What a lovely surprise. Didn't expect to see you today." She stank of a sickly-sweet perfume that was over generously applied. "For me?" she said as he proffered the flowers. "What have I done to deserve these?"

Craig just smiled, saying nothing.

She waved him in, making her way along the hall toward the kitchen. "Can't believe tomorrow's your big day."

"Where's Dad?" he asked, ignoring her comment.

"Round the back. Tinkering on his car, as usual. I'll go fetch him, shall I?"

"No need. I'll go say hello in a bit."

166

She entered the kitchen, putting the flowers in the sink and turned her back on him as she began trimming the stalks.

"How's the flat?"

"Fine."

"Enjoying your independence?" She could barely disguise the disgust in her voice, which amused him greatly.

"Sure." He stuck his hand into his pocket, stroking and feeling the leather strap. He'd sneaked it out of his parents' wardrobe years ago and had kept it with him ever since. Originally it was to stop her from using it on him.

"Does Dad still have his old pistol upstairs?"

She cocked her head slightly. "Why on earth would you ask that?"

"Just remember seeing it as a kid, that's all."

She returned to the task of trimming the flowers. "I suppose it's up there somewhere."

He drew the strap out of his pocket, then moved quickly behind her, slipping it around her neck, hearing a series of animalistic grunts and snorts escape her. She squirmed and struggled against him, repeatedly kicking the cabinet door. Finally, she stopped fighting. He untangled the strap and watched her slump heavily to the floor.

He kicked her…

…and saw himself down there, hands raised, yelling, crying out as Mum beat him with the strap, her fleshy face flushed, livid and contorted.

"How dare you call my father that!" she screamed. "How dare you! How dare you speak about your grandfather that way!"

167

Craig wandered out into the garden, spying Dad inside his garage, bent over the front of his grey Morris Minor. An assortment of car parts and tools lay scattered around his feet.

Craig stooped, snatching up a claw hammer.

Had Dad always been so quick to accept Mum's family, he wondered? Perhaps he had been propelled by demons of his own; after all, they say like attracts like.

Craig moved swiftly, keenly, behind him, raising the hammer before driving it down hard onto the back of his father's head. Dad staggered forward, groaning, flailing his arms. Craig landed further blows, one after the other, beating his father mercilessly to the ground.

There was blood in Craig's eyes; he had to wipe it away to see:

...himself back inside the house, considerably younger, smaller. He was dressed in pyjamas and slippers; his father had seen him up and about using the bathroom only moments before and was now calling for him from inside his parents' bedroom.

Craig shuffled slowly into the room, then froze – sick to the very bottom of his stomach at the sight before him.

"Close the door," his father instructed. "Go stand in the corner. Watch. Do as I say. Under this roof, we hide nothing from each other."

He did as he was told, staring at the naked forms on the bed, moving, twisting, fusing.

Skin pressing against skin.

Laughter.

168

Whispers.

Pants, groans.

Two as one.

A meld of glistening flesh…

***

It was late. Close to midnight. A full moon hovered spectrally over the roofs of the housing estate. Craig sat in contemplative silence, allowing a succession of memories to flood him. Of setting up armies of toy soldiers in his and his brother's room, despite Andy being a little too old for the game. Trading jokes and whispering to each other after lights out. Andy sharing a cigarette with him outside the school gates when he was fourteen.

He rubbed his eyes, the memories dissipating instantly.

He grabbed a cannister in the footwell, then clambered out of the car. Closed the driver's-side door and pulled the hood of his jacket up over his head. He crossed the road, avoiding the streetlamp's glow. The windows of his brother's house were smothered with darkness; there was no sign of anyone up. Petrol syphoned from Dad's Morris Minor sloshed around inside the cannister.

He paused, glancing up and down the street. Good, he thought: *no one around*. He stared at the living room window, seeing his own face float in a sea of blackness.

Andy lived with his two boys, Sam, aged 6 and Jonathan, aged 5. Andy was a fair few years older than Craig, but they'd always been close. Until Andy got baptised, of course.

Craig hurriedly twisted off the top of the cannister, spreading the petrol around inside the porch and then splashing it up the walls. He lit a match, threw it. Turned and ran for cover.

He reached his car, leapt inside. Pulled the door closed and slunk down, hearing the flames outside roar.

The street suddenly lit up, people out shouting and screaming…

…but Craig was sat on a bench with Andy in the park, watching Jonathan and Sam play together on a climbing frame.

Andy was smiling at him. "I'm honestly doing okay," he said. "I don't think about Marie at all now. I've come to realise that she wasn't the one. She wouldn't accept us. Any of us. And family's important, right?"

Craig said nothing, his hands thrust deep into the pockets of his jacket.

"I still have the boys. She was never going to take them away from me."

Craig remained silent, mulling this over.

"What are you thinking?" Andy asked.

Craig shrugged. Then, very quietly, he said: "What happens down there, Andy?"

Andy turned away, watching his kids charge around the climbing frame. Then, turning back, meeting Craig's gaze again, he shrugged and replied, "They lock you down there and the darkness just fills you up. That's all there is to it."

"What is it that's down there, Andy?"

170

"It needs us," Andy said, ignoring the question, urgency building in his voice. "Then we need it. We all feel better in the dark, Craig."

Craig looked toward Andy's children on the climbing frame.

He was shaking like a leaf.

"Your boys," he whispered. "Will you let the same thing happen to them?"

***

Craig arrived at the base of the hill just after sunrise. He got out of the car, thrust his hood up, and climbed the hill.

Grandad's place awaited him at the top, looking almost serene under the slats of early morning sunlight. There was scaffolding up and land cleared away around it, all ready for the extension.

The front door was unlocked. Craig pushed on through, entering the hall. The stairs faced him, leading up to a deserted landing. To his right was Grandad's large sitting room. Craig reached into his jacket pocket, touching and stroking cold metal.

Grandad was in the sitting room, seated in his armchair with his back to Craig. He was an early riser; awake with the sparrow's fart, as he used to say.

Craig waited a few contemplative seconds, telling himself *I can finish this*. Then, breathing out quietly, slowly, he wandered across into his grandfather's line of sight and flicked off the TV.

"Who…?" Grandad began, jolting, sitting bolt upright in his seat.

The outraged expression on Grandad's face softened. "Craig?"

"Hi, Grandad."

Craig grabbed a stool by the TV, sitting himself on it, staring his grandfather hard in the eye.

I'm not afraid of you anymore, he thought.

"What are you doing here?"

"Thought I'd come early." Craig managed to project a smile. "It's my big day, remember? My eighteenth birthday. The time when I'm finally supposed to accept all this, right?"

Grandad nodded vaguely, his eyes betraying his suspicion. "Your parents here?"

Craig shook his head.

Grandad threw a glance at the door beneath the stairs.

Craig looked, too. Then, reaching deep inside his jacket pocket, he carefully extracted Dad's Luger.

"Craig…" Grandad began, waving his hand vigorously in the air.

Craig cocked the gun, pointing it directly at the old man.

"Craig," Grandad said again, showing him his palms in what appeared to be a gesture of utter desperation. "It's *all* good, okay? Once it's done, you'll realise. You'll *see*. Just… just understand that…"

"Bye."

A bullet tore right through Grandad's face, knocking the old man back into his chair, his body sliding down the seat to flop brokenly over the armrest. A thread of smoke coiled lazily up to the ceiling from the crown of Grandad's head. Craig stood up and put three more bullets into him.

He lowered his arm, puffed out his cheeks. Looked about…

…and saw his family congregated around him inside this very room. But there was someone missing – and very quickly he turned his body toward the cellar door.

Andy.

The door was shut tight.

Mum and Dad were sitting on the sofa, hand-in-hand, their expressions one of strange joy and pride. Grandad had his hands on Craig, his long, nicotine-stained fingers gripping and kneading Craig's arms.

Andy was kicking and punching the cellar door, screaming at the top of his lungs.

"It comes part and parcel with being a member of this family," Grandad explained. "We accept it because of the love we share and the traditions we carry."

Craig wanted to wriggle free and help his brother, but Grandad held him hard and fast and wouldn't let go.

"It's what being a family's about. All things suffered and shared, young man. And that," he nodded at the cellar door, "is what binds us all together."

Craig blinked back into the present moment.

He sat down again on the stool, gazing at the twisted, curled-up form of his grandfather. He closed his eyes and heard a soft *click* come from the other side of the room. He opened his eyes, looked across the room at the cellar door.

It was standing open now, revealing flickering, unfolding strands of a strange and sentient darkness.

If he wasn't going in, he realised, then it was going to have to come out for him.

He watched the darkness invade the room, weaving and coiling into the air, shimmering before him like a heat haze. He felt it wind itself around him, pressing up close, emitting a series of eerie whistling and howling sounds. He could see it clearer now, a little better – snake-like, vapor-like, consisting of swirling black wisps, tendrils, and tongues.

Craig slammed shut his eyes.

Let it in some, he thought. Just enough, and…

His fingers tightened around Dad's pistol.

The darkness was infiltrating him now, passing through his mouth and nostrils, corrupting him and all that he could ever be. He felt it fight against his intense revulsion, trying, cannily, to normalise itself within him.

He wasn't going to let that happen.

He lifted the gun and pressed its muzzle tight against his temple. Seconds later he squeezed the trigger, purifying the darkness, purging it with fleeting, searing light, consigning his family's twisted secrets and traditions to the oblivion they deserved.

174

You Give Me Fever

from notes by Joel Lane

It didn't take long to find her. Gossips in shabby pubs directed me to Ecos Court where a loose-tongued neighbour disclosed Mary's flat number. I thanked the neighbour, took the lift up to the second floor and drifted along a corridor to her pale, unpainted door.

Winter was loosening its grip on me – warmth and sensation spread through my frame as I rapped at the letterbox. I tugged my coat collar, suddenly feeling nauseous and out of breath. Without warning, the door jolted open and a security chain snapped taut.

"Please," I said, splaying out my hand against the door. "Please, Mary. I just want to talk."

A strangled cry came from within and I wondered if the shock might be enough to kill her. Then I took my hand away and the door slammed on me. "Mary? Mary … *please*."

I stopped calling to her after a while and tilted my head forward so that it rested against the door. I stood very still, breathing hard against wood. In my head I saw dirty creases in the air, black lines moving toward me. I smiled briefly, emptily to myself. Then the door jerked open and I seized the doorframe to avoid falling at her feet.

She'd gone back inside but had taken the chain off its hook. I shuffled forward, scuffing the soles of my shoes on a doormat. There were some wooden steps leading up to a room that was just out of sight.

175

I took them carefully, the treads creaking and complaining beneath me, my hand gripping a loose rail as I ascended.

I edged into the sitting room just as the old woman was easing herself into an armchair next to the window. I caught a glimpse of myself in the glass and, as usual, convinced myself it was him looking in on things, appealing in vain for acceptance and companionship – a distant echo of my own pitiable existence in this world.

Her Gorgon stare fixed me and I quickly looked away, trying to seek a trace of the familiar within the room. Weirdly, I thought of the pornography Aiden had written about – stuff she used to make him watch – but there was none of that here. Perhaps it was stored in a drawer somewhere, or perhaps it was long gone, destroyed in a fit of panic when the authorities had pounced. I began to recall details of our house back in Bristol. Paisley wallpaper. Tall windows shuttered against the sunlight. That splintered door beneath the stairs. The half-formed things in jars in the cellar…

"Well, this is a surprise," she said, interrupting my thoughts, squirming in her seat as I perched myself on the sofa. "Didn't think I'd see you again. Thought I'd found a place to escape everything. Guess I thought wrong." She rubbed her eye vigorously with a fist. "The date's not lost on me, you know. If I'd have known you were coming, I might've got something in. We could have had a celebration." She laughed mirthlessly at her words.

The air was thick and uncomfortably hot. A film of sweat broke out across my forehead. I thought about taking my coat off but I didn't want to forget it and leave it here. I wished I was outside, in the cold, anesthetised by winter once more.

"Why this year?" Her grey eyes glittered with distrust. "You want answers? Is that it?" Her expression mutated into a maniacal mask of contempt. "We breathed life into you, Martin. *Both* of you. But it was too much … especially for your father's wretched conscience." She laughed another humourless laugh, then waved her hand dismissively as she tugged her cardigan around her shoulders. "It wasn't that I preferred Aiden, of course. I just wasn't allowed to keep you both. Perhaps in hindsight I made the wrong decision, considering…" She pulled in a breath. "Still, you were given to a good home, right? Given to people who accepted you for what you are. Probably better off where…"

"I don't want answers." I shook my head, cutting her off mid-sentence, sweat flicking off my face. "This isn't about me."

"Then what is this about?" Her cheekbones twitched as she gripped the armrests and straightened in her chair, her wizened fragility disappearing before my eyes. "There's nothing for you here. There never was!"

I noticed a picture standing on top of the bookcase, one that wasn't grey and made up of flecks.

I got to my feet, snatched it up. He looked about fifteen, a shy, strained smile creasing his face. There was more than a hint of sadness to that expression, I felt.

177

"After his father died, he was all I had." She nodded at it, her voice drained of emotion. "It was his madness, not mine. It always was."

I briefly closed my eyes, my heart hammering away inside of me.

I remember reading about the diary the detectives had found in his flat: a vicious, hate-filled thing that became more violent and rambling as it went on, frequently name-dropping Mary and all her terrible misdemeanours.

I opened my eyes, sighed, and stood the picture back up on the bookcase.

She was talking again but I wasn't listening anymore. I could smell formaldehyde and was opening the splintered door beneath the stairs…

I wished we'd stayed down there now. Wished we'd never been made to leave that womb of dust and darkness.

Above all else, I wished we'd never been separated, Aiden and I.

He was the only one who could have known what it's like to be me.

Mary's voice was raised now, her words betraying her madness; a madness that became Aiden's reality and filled him with a fever there could be no recovery from, no cure for…

"…not a child, no. More like a sick animal, a sick dog. And then he wanted us to make him a girl, a female companion; something to fuck, I suppose. He wasn't right in the head. We should have aborted before we even attempted to…" She shook her head viciously. "He was filled with such uncertainty and self-pity. Took after his father for that, I suppose.

178

And the ironic thing was, they both went the same way – knotting their hospital bedding into nooses and then leaving me here to face a barrage of unwanted attention *all on my own*." Her wizened claws bunched into fists in her lap. "And the business with the whores … those three women *he* butchered that night, validating my belief he was a mistake, that we should never have made him."

I sat down and stared at her wild-eyed form. Remembered the newspapers, the TV reports; the widespread horror and condemnation of him.

"…and he wrote it was *me*," she prodded at herself with a finger. "The *poison* of my body and mind, infecting *his* world. Couldn't he see I was trying to *protect* him? Toughening him up so he could grow into the man he *needed* to be?"

Spit exploded from her mouth as she gloated about having never been incriminated or sectioned, but I was tuning out of her paranoid diatribe.

Survival through denial. Mary was an adept.

I was burning up, sweat trickling down my brow to soak and sting my eyes. I glanced round and saw the radiator beside me, tapping it first with my knuckles before gripping it with my fingers. Cold. I breathed and saw vapour, yet my body was bathed in sweat.

I stared at Mary, clouds of mist escaping her lips as she glared at me with eyes of ice and fire, then allowed my gaze to slide across to the figure framed in the windowpane beside her. "It wasn't your fault," I whispered and offered him the scantest of smiles. "Not really."

I often think it should have been me. Not him.

And the guilt never goes away – no matter how often I try telling myself it hadn't been my fault, that I'd been too young and powerless to have ever been able to change anything.

I spoke then and the words which tumbled from my lips were distant and unreal, like when your sinuses are blocked and your own voice sounds like a ghost chattering in your ear: "I have a love in me that you can scarcely imagine."

I found my feet, disgust and panic exploding across her face. I sank to my knees and opened my arms out wide.

"Hold me, Mother." That made her wince and I laughed, meekly. "It's all I've ever wanted."

She tried to bat me away but I wrapped my arms around her and pulled her in close. In a bid to connect to something, anything, I craned my head forward and focused on the mug beside her. My sullen reflection rippled on the surface of her tea, gaunt and feral-looking in the pale-brown liquid. Except it wasn't my face; it was *his* face, getting clearer and stronger all the time, like a photograph in developing fluid. And he was grinning, nodding his head with approval as I squeezed.

She began to squirm and thrash but I hugged her fiercer, tighter, enveloping her. My left hand gripped the wrist of my right arm, squeezing with all my might until I heard a bone crack and an animal sound escape her.

I kept hugging and twisting until the tears and the sweat were streaming down my face and my eyes were filled with bright, hallucinatory patterns. I swallowed a scream and ground my teeth together,

180

squeezing even harder. In time I let go and she sagged like a doll in my arms. My head felt as though it was on fire. I stood unsteadily, bumping into the wall as she slipped off her armchair to fall in a heap on the floor. She looked deformed and twisted on the carpet, like something she and Dad might have conceived in their make-shift laboratory before the police and social services intervened. I kicked her. She didn't move.

I turned, walked out the room and trudged downstairs with sweat dripping from my trembling body. I stumbled along the corridor and pushed through the communal door into the courtyard outside. The beads of sweat on my forehead joined and became trickling rivulets of coldness down my cheeks. I scurried out the main gates and kept walking without aim or purpose until I'd stopped perspiring and my heart had slowed to its normal rate. Soon winter's chill reached my bones and I was so desperately glad. I could see the cold again as dirty creases in the air, black lines moving toward me. Something flickered in the corner of my vision. I whirled, focused and beheld a shape twitching upon the surface of a shadowy shop window.

We were cut from the same cloth – we'd always looked similar – so it's easy to imagine he's here, still around, and I'm not alone in this world.

"Happy birthday."

The words left me in a plume of vapour. Our strained smiles slipped from our faces as the illusion of him began to fade. Then I turned and hurried on, into the anesthetising cold, eager not to feel anything but numb again.

Lesson In The Eternal School

with John B. Ford

The appearance of Wainscroft High School reflected an air of prolonged decay that appeared to have spread from the crumbling stonework of the building to infect the minds of teachers and pupils alike. Situated six miles from the nearest Peak District town of Glossop, its low attendance by pupils was outdone only by its pitiable results in the government established Ofsted league tables. It was inconceivable how such a quality of neglect had been allowed to manifest in this day and age, when building safety standards and educational quality were of paramount importance to the continued functioning of any school.

Each morning brought fewer pupils on the local buses that wound their way up the narrow lanes across the bleak moorlands of heather and cold gritstone rock. Even the drivers of these vehicles seemed filled with a melancholic reluctance to make their routine journeys to Wainscroft.

It was one of these single deck buses that carried Thomas Diole, a government school inspector who had been recently assigned to investigating the poor results of the school. When he had heard about the possible closure of the school he had taken a personal interest, not just for the sake of the pupils and their education, but because thirty years previously he had lived in the area and attended Wainscroft High School himself.

At the time the standard of education in the school had been exemplary and his own examination results had paved the way for his enrolment at Oxford University. There was no doubt that he wouldn't have attained the job he was doing now if it hadn't been for the excellent start in life the school had provided.

Diole had taken an early train from Manchester's Piccadilly Station to Glossop. Upon his arrival at the station there he walked over to the adjacent car park, showed his identity card to the apathetic driver of a waiting school bus, and was admitted in silence. He noticed, with some surprise, that the bus seemed not dissimilar to the one he used to catch thirty years back, the main difference being there was only a dozen or so pupils seated inside.

The mood of these adolescents was in marked contrast to anything Diole had known before. Their faces were sullen and wan, showing no sign at all of the vitality and exuberance usually inherent in that age group. Nor was there any conversation between the pupils, as though they had nothing in common but their destination and an ill-favoured summons.

The bus departed from the car park and soon left the main streets of Glossop behind to enter the wilder moorland country of Longdendale and beyond. A blanket of thick fog hung low over the narrow road they now travelled upon, causing the driver to reduce his speed and travel more warily. Diole remembered the areas of marshland that formed after periods of heavy rain; the roads close proximity to them had always been a concern but

183

never to an extent that it should prevent pupils from making the journey to school. If Wainscroft offered this as any part of their excuse for low attendance the team of inspectors would have to reject it. The other members in the team were all based in Sheffield and thus had arranged to share two cars and travel to the school via the Snake Pass, another treacherous road at the best of times.

As the bus continued to make its slow progress, Diole noticed small clouds of black smoke hanging over the seats occupied by the pupils. He recalled cigarettes had been popular with many of his peers during his time at Wainscroft but was appalled to find the filthy habit still took place, especially when the government had recently banned it from all enclosed public places. The drivers of school buses should enforce such laws; Diole had no choice but to take out his notepad and scribble a memo to confront the headteacher about the matter.

When he'd finished writing and looked up again he was appalled to find a cloud of smoke had drifted over to him. He wafted it with his pad but it only made matters worse and the smell became an acrid stench, reminding him of a hospital crematorium he had once walked too close to. His vision blurred and he suddenly felt unwell.

***

Diole was jolted awake as the bus came to a halt outside the school gates. He had no memory of drifting off to sleep, and his head ached as though he'd recently been knocked unconscious. He looked around suspiciously but saw only the same few blank-faced pupils languidly filtering off the bus. Getting up from his seat, Diole began to follow them.

The bus driver looked up quizzically from the newspaper rested on his steering wheel when Diole began to speak to him.

"Haven't you heard about the recent government law banning smoking from enclosed public places?" he asked, an edgy bitterness present in his voice.

"Course I have, mate, an' if you ask me it's a bloody stupid law! Nobody ever used to complain when folk smoked at the back of my bus – if you ask me it never hurt anyone a bit. Nowadays if just one bloke's travellin' alone on one of my runs an' he lights up a fag, I have to stop the bus an' shout back an' tell him to put it out. It comes difficult to me since I'm a big smoker an all."

"So why did you allow the children on the bus to smoke this morning?"

"What're you talkin' 'bout, mate? I just told you I can't allow anyone at all to smoke these days. I just told you that."

"I distinctly saw smoke hanging over their seats, it even drifted over to me and I was unfortunate enough to inhale it."

"You saw nowt of the kind, mate! Maybe you got confused by all that fog outside, or perhaps some of it came in if a kid opened a slide-window, that's all."

"I know fog when I see it," replied Diole, "and what I saw in the bus today was no fog. I'll be mentioning this when I speak to the headteacher presently, and I'll expect him to be in touch with your superiors."

Sudden anger flashed in the eyes of the driver as he threw his newspaper aside and began to stand up.

"Nobody calls me a liar, you pompous bastard! I'm not much bothered about this bleedin' job anymore and you know somethin'… to break your fuckin' nose would be an ideal way to go out!"

A genuine wave of fear passed through Diole as he quickly exited the bus, half expecting the driver to come after him. He'd not been threatened with violence since his own school days here at Wainscroft; his role as head prefect had made him a target for the bullies in the same year as him and he'd ended up paying them 'protection money' to keep his teeth intact. Diole's remembrance of this made him angry and ashamed he'd given way to their demands out of fear and without any attempt of resistance.

As he walked beyond the rusted iron gates and into the schoolyard, Diole was taken aback by the notable lack of pupils in attendance; from a quick look around he estimated there to be less than one hundred present. However, not only was it the dearth of pupils that bothered him, it was also the languid demeanour of those that had bothered to turn up. They stood around in small groups, all of them hunched over with their hands in their pockets and their eyes aimed at the ground, and each of them appearing as devoid of life as the school itself.

If one studied the building there was no sign of maintenance taking place at all, with areas of cracked or crumbling stonework bringing safety issues to the forefront, while most of the windows appeared so grimy they'd obviously never been cleaned in years. A look up at the black slate roof showed areas where years of buffeting winds had dislodged tiles, while in others they had been utterly ripped off and cast down to the ground where the cracked remains had been left untouched.

Diole was further mystified when he looked over at the allocated car parking area for staff and visitors and saw that every space was still vacant. In fact its neglected state made it appear like it was never used; in many areas weeds had broken through the tarmac surface and flourished to the extent they obscured the faded white lines designating the spaces. Perhaps the teachers as well as most of the pupils never bothered turning up, he thought wryly.

Just then his reverie was interrupted when the school bell rang and the listless pupils began filing into the building via the two main entrance doors. Though there still wasn't any sign of the rest of the inspection team arriving, Diole decided that he should enter the school without them and, if he *could* locate any of the teaching staff, explain to them the procedure of the inspection due to take place.

He began to feel unwell soon after he followed the last few pupils through the entrance doors, but put his queasiness down to a putrid odour that hung within the air of the building. It reminded him of the incident of the pupils smoking on the school bus, and this caused him, once again, to think of the stench of a crematorium.

In the large reception area the children were now shuffling through an arched doorway, their eyes dull, glassy and downturned. A tall man in a suit and tie was busy talking to two adults in a corner, smiling intermittently and amicably at them. Diole listened in, realising the adults were parents of a child from the school.

"…hasn't been himself for a while," the father mumbled, his face gaunt and unshaven, his brows furrowed with concern.

"He's been very down," nodded the mother, her hair lank-looking and prematurely grey. "His mood is affecting us all. Me. Des, here. His two brothers…"

The man in the suit – who Diole now took to be a member of staff – made sweeping, placating gestures with his hands. "I'm sure it's just a phase," he soothed. "Lots of changes are occurring inside that young man, and low mood and introspection are common in boys his age, I'm afraid."

Diole noted the lack of a handrail on the stairs, the scuffed and frayed rug, the cobwebs covering the ceiling and walls. His face scrunched up in disgust.

The parents were leaving now, heading for the exit, walking away slowly with their heads down. "Ah," cried the teacher, striding over to Diole, his robe flapping around him. "You must be one of the inspectors. How marvellous!"

Diole wondered if the teacher was being sarcastic. "My name's Mr. Diole and I am indeed one of the inspectors. Who are you, may I ask?"

The man thrust out a hand, which Diole reluctantly shook. "Mr. Vochel, headteacher here at Wainscroft High." There was something about the man's smile, and the clamminess of his hand, that set Diole's teeth on edge. "Care for the grand tour, Mr. Diole?"

"That won't strictly be necessary, headteacher. Being an ex-student, I know Wainscroft like the back of my own hand." His gaze scanned the peeling wallpaper; the worn treads; the dusty main desk. "Very little has changed in all this time, I see."

Mr. Vochel seemed unruffled, continuing to hold his abominably wide and bright smile high up on his face. "An ex-pupil, eh? How apt."

"Where are the rest of the staff?"

"Gathering the pupils together for morning assembly."

Diole chewed his lip, then uttered with some annoyance: "The rest of the Ofsted team should be here any minute now, so I'd like to crack on, please." That putrid odour returned, invading his nostrils and causing his face to twist into an involuntary grimace. "I must say, my initial impressions of the school are far from good."

Even that had failed to wipe the nauseating smile from off the headteacher's face. "Your concerns will be allayed, Mr. Diole." He gestured toward the arched doorway with a wave of his hand. "Come with me and observe our morning assembly.

We'll turn your opinion of us around in no time, old boy."

Diole muttered under his breath as he followed the headteacher through the doorway into a narrow, gloomy stairwell. They paused at the top of a steep set of metal stairs. "Down here?" Diole exclaimed. "Surely not!" Disgust and incredulity mingled upon his face. "This doesn't seem appropriate in the slightest. Why are the children down *there?* That's the basement, if my memory serves me right."

"You're quite correct, Mr. Diole." Mr. Vochel's tone was glib and vaguely patronising.

"And these stairs – well, health and safety would have a field day!"

Diole continued to mutter away to himself as he inched downwards, the soles of his shoes ringing on the steps like sad bells. Where were his colleagues? What on Earth was taking them so long?

A wooden door awaited him at the bottom which, when pushed, opened out onto a large, candle-lit room. Diole coughed, wrinkling his nose. The stench was far worse down here.

"Go on in," Mr. Vochel urged. "That's it, don't be shy!"

Diole shot Vochel a look, then slipped into the room and surveyed his surroundings.

Some of the children were here, sat in a semi-circle in front of a blank wall-mounted projector screen. Long, crooked shadows striped the floor, reminding Diole of a German expressionist film he'd once had the misfortune of sitting through. Even more disturbing were the grotesqueries positioned around the room – coffins standing open and empty; human skulls leering obscenely from the shadows; fully assembled skeletons in cages hanging suspended from the ceiling.

Gathered around the children were adults shrouded from head to foot in black, their veils barely concealing their taut, maniacal grins.

"What on…?" Diole frantically wheeled, the blood rushing to his face. "It's hardly Halloween, Mr. Vochel!" The dark-shrouded adults lifted their heads, turned and gazed at Diole through their silken veils. Diole's panicked eyes flinched toward them again. "I-I don't understand…"

The words stalled inside his mouth as one of the shrouded figures stepped forward, announcing to everyone: "Today it's Michael's turn." Diole noticed the blank-eyed schoolboy standing silent in the corner. "He's ready and waiting to embrace his transition. What *all* of us are resigned to in the end."

Michael shuffled forward, the other children putting their hands together and applauding in a strange, spiritless fashion. The boy sat as soon as the clapping stopped, lifting his face up toward the screen. Diole thought he saw wisps of smoke coil from the child's hands as he folded them together on his lap.

Mr. Vochel closed the basement door, glancing up at the overhead projector as it rumbled into life.

Diole, growing increasingly fretful and frightened, blinked and focused his attention on the projector screen, too.

An old monochrome documentary started playing – black and white footage of filmed and

191

photographed events: a series of horrific World War II atrocities; shots of Nazi concentration camps; the Zapruder film of the Kennedy assassination; images of the self-immolation of Thích Quảng Đức; victims at violent crime scenes; Victorian after-death pictures commemorating the dead.

"What is this, some kind of sick joke?" Diole spat, his fingers tugging anxiously at his shirt collar.

Michael continued staring at the screen while the other children turned their heads and gazed lifelessly at Diole.

"All is one with darkness," they intoned. "All is one with the void."

"What...?" Diole began, but he couldn't finish; it was as if his tongue had swelled up in his mouth.

"This is about *permanence*, Mr. Diole." Mr. Vochel had dropped his voice to a low whisper: "Anything else that's taught is a lie, delivered merely to divert and deflect from *The Truth of All Things*." Black smoke was beginning to rise from Michael's juddering, convulsing body.

"In Wainscroft," Mr. Vochel continued, "we understand and respect the truth. We'd be deceitful if we planted false hopes and promises inside these small humans."

The basement's acrid stench was fast becoming intolerable, reminding Diole, once more, of that hospital crematorium. The children meanwhile continued to stare at Diole as sparks danced and flickered across the whole of Michael's body.

Diole felt his legs begin to buckle beneath him, his life flashing before his eyes as he wobbled and swayed:

He was a boy again, wearing Wainscroft's uniform, so eager and desperate to please. He saw himself in the school playground, being picked on by other children, his feelings of exclusion festering, growing; slowly shaping him into the insular and distrustful man he would later become.

Michael suddenly exploded into a ball of white fire, but Diole was oblivious.

Everything I've done, he thought, *everything I've achieved is all but an empty charade. My life is a floating speck in an expanding, inhospitable universe. There is only truth in accepting the void…*

The adults began to clap from behind the folds of their cloaks.

Diole, meanwhile, lost command of his senses, collapsing to the floor in a heap after falling unconscious.

***

He came to at last, coughing, groaning, a thick string of saliva dangling from his lips. He sat up, groggily squinting into the crooked shadows of the room. The candles remained lit, but he appeared alone – abandoned on the floor of the basement with only the dark for company.

At last, he thought, gazing at the tiny black sparks dancing upon his hands. I realise. I *understand.*

He was like the staff. The children.

A message.

An emissary.

Everything else was false… Futile, even.

Two leather shoes scuffed forward, stopping abruptly before him.

I'll be able to teach and instruct others, he thought as a black cloth was cast over his body, darkening his world further. *Starting very soon with…*

He looked up at Mr. Vochel's downturned face through the folds and crinkles of his shroud. Then, as the headteacher spoke, Diole delivered him a taut, maniacal grin.

"The other inspectors have arrived!"

Until The Light Takes Us

Part I

"Cam, listen.

"I've moved to a higher plateau. I'm beyond flesh now.

"One person, one person alone means nothing. We can change, really we can, but we have to evolve and expand.

"Cam...listen. I've seen another world.

"Let me take you."

July, 1994

The man parked his Escort in a layby, then killed the car's engine.

Sunflowers rustled. Birds shrilled. A dead yew raised twisted arms to the sky, as if in praise of the oncoming night.

He stared into the rear-view mirror, contemplating the three little girls in the back. Their wide eyes shimmered with worry, fear and confusion. He felt for them. Wanted so badly to save them.

Too late.

He opened the car door.

"Daddy?"

"Shush," he whispered.

He closed the car door, then approached the chapel by the side of the road. He went inside, swiftly disappearing into thick, dust-choked darkness.

For a while, there was silence; it was as though the world was holding its breath. Finally he re-emerged, looking dazed and confused, his eyes shining in the dreamy, purplish twilight.

He returned to the car, opened up the back-passenger door. Knelt down and faced the first little girl.

In her eyes he saw his own face shimmer, tremble and shine.

"You have to do something for me." He gripped the girl's hand, smoothing it, squeezing it. "I want you to go in that chapel." He looked at the other girls. "All of you. One at a time."

The first little girl began to cry. "I don't want to, Daddy."

"You must." He lifted her from the car. "It's for your own good."

The first girl walked uncertainly away, glancing fretfully over her shoulder as she advanced, the chapel looming over her like a silent bird of doom.

May, 2014

In the dark of their flat, Megan and Cameron watched the late evening news together. It was filled with the usual stories of death, misery and despair.

A couple had blown themselves up in a restaurant in Djibouti. Boko Haram had pillaged three villages in Borno State, killing twenty-eight people and kidnapping many more. Ten people had been killed in an attack by al-Shabab on the parliament building in Somalia. Twenty-seven dead following an overnight raid on Yemeni government buildings in Seiyun.

"Christ," Cameron whispered, shaking his head from side-to-side.

"What?" Megan looked up and around, eyebrows raised, face pale in the darkness.

"The world's gone crazy. How can people claiming to be human beings murder people like this?"

"They don't think they're doing anything wrong." She crushed her hands together in her lap. "Far from it. In fact, they fervently believe it's right."

"It's fucking scary."

"Huh," she said. "I've never known you to get like this before."

"Like what?"

She nodded at the TV. "Current affairs, the news... What's all that got to do with you? Us?"

Cameron straightened in his seat. "It's got everything to do with us. I mean..." He frowned. "Are you upset with me?"

"No." She vigorously rubbed her eyes. "Not upset. Just... disappointed, I guess. Didn't Beth say you were a closed book? You've changed, Cam."

He felt the skin crawl over the bone of his scalp. "Doesn't any of this worry you? I mean, the war in Syria..."

"We've all got our wars to fight." She spoke the words through gritted teeth. "In here." She tapped her head with her forefinger. "Out there."

She nodded in the direction of the window. "Everything needs fixing. None of it's right. Just ripples for the cataclysm to come."

He tried to take in the implication of her words. "I'm not saying we're perfect. I know our own lives and systems are flawed…"

"It needs tearing down and starting again," she snapped, her face twisting into a grotesque mask of hate. "Everything's decaying. Everything's wrong."

He sensed the walls shimmer strangely around him. She got up and left the room, slamming the door on her way out.

July, 2014

Cameron and Megan heaved their luggage into the hotel, straightened and let the rain slip down their tired, shivering faces. Cameron knuckled his eyes, eager to grab some much-needed sleep.

The lobby was half-lit by two green lamps, one on a wooden table by the door, the other on the reception desk next to a vase of freshly cut flowers. To their left, a staircase curled away into darkness.

"Blast." Megan dragged a hand through her hair. "I've left our overnight bag in the car."

"I'll get it." Cameron zipped up his coat. "You sort out the room."

He slipped back out of the hotel, rain crackling against his mac. He sprinted to Meg's Clio, swung open the front passenger door. Waited for a lightning flash to help locate the bag in the footwell. Moments later he was back inside, pulling the hotel doors closed behind him.

The lobby was deserted, Megan gone.

Behind the seething rain, Cameron could hear the faint hum of the lamps and the lonesome tick of the long-case clock in the corner.

"*Bon soir.*"

He wheeled, seeing a tall, willowy woman standing behind the wood panelled reception desk.

"*Votre ami est à l'étage,*" she said.

He blinked twice, rapidly.

She sighed, then nodded toward the staircase.

"Up here?" he said, pointing.

"*Oui. A l'étage.*"

He quickly climbed the stairs, then drifted along the first floor landing. Doors reared up around him, shadows pirouetted across walls. Two more green lamps shone, one on a bookcase, the other on a table and right at the end of the landing a window glowed every so often with reflected lightning.

He came upon a door that was ajar. He pressed against it, pushed hard. To his relief, Megan was inside, standing dead-still in front of a window.

He thought of the time in the Residents' Centre when her eyes had shone in that dark, back room.

"Meg?"

She threw a glance at him and he was relieved to see her eyes weren't shining now.

"Thanks," he huffed, kicking shut the door. "I really appreciate it when you run off like that."

Her gaze flicked back to the window. "Shush. Come and look. The storm's fantastic."

Blinding lights. Destructive forces. These things sang in her bones and burned through her veins.

199

He dumped the bag on the dressing table, then sat down on the bed behind her. The room was whitewashed, sparsely decorated. A wooden chair lurked in a corner, shrouded in darkness.

She reached out, lightly touching his knee. "What's the matter?"

"Why did you leave me like that?" He pulled off his coat. "The woman downstairs *talked* to me, Meg."

She tossed her head back and laughed, loudly.

"It's goddamn hot," he muttered, clawing at his shirt collar. "I thought the storm might clear the air." He winced at the irritation underscoring his words. The fear of the unknown, the anxiety of being in an unfamiliar place where he didn't speak the same language was all beginning to grate. "I find it difficult to communicate at the best of times," he said, not meaning to say it out loud.

Megan flashed him a strange, sad smile. "It's what you carry around inside that counts. We'll all get to express ourselves soon. *Then* people shall know."

Her eyes slowly filled with that mysterious light as a clap of thunder rattled the fragile silence of the room.

December, 2013

Cameron's heart was beating fast and there was a flutter of butterflies in his stomach. He was stood outside the Residents' Centre, mulling over how he'd come to be here. He remembered the card,

200

viewed three days ago; stuck to the centre's window by pieces of Blu-Tack.

If you feel angry, lost, or scared, you're not alone. Come to our meetings – 7pm every Wednesday at the Residents' Centre, St. John's Road, Frome.

His mind projected images of his flat – empty, silent, and dark – and that had decided it; he didn't want to be alone again tonight.

Drawing breath, he opened the door and stepped tentatively inside.

The room was bright and inviting. Furniture and play equipment had been pushed to one side. Sat in a circle in the middle of the room were six people who all looked up and around as he entered.

"H-hi," he stammered, raising his hand.

A bearded man with sharp grey eyes quickly rose, a nervous smile playing around the corners of his mouth. "Come in," he said, lifting a chair from off a stack in the corner. "You're here for the group, right?"

"Yes." Cameron nodded, feeling the colour rise to his cheeks.

"Good. Oh, good." Relief passed across the man's face. "Please sit."

Cameron sat.

The man sank into the chair opposite him, then leapt up again, offering Cameron his hand. "I'm Patrick."

"Cameron."

"Nice to meet you, Cameron."

201

They shook hands, and Patrick sat back down. The guy seemed filled with nervous, infectious energy.

"Stephanie." Patrick turned to a young woman to his left. "Please, continue. You were saying?"

The woman tucked a strand of blonde hair behind her ear, throwing a cautious glance at Cameron. She shut her eyes briefly before saying, "It's a power point in Rennes-le-Château. We know there are others – power distilled from the Ark and then contained within walls. And there are more containers now; walking carriers – the power contained in flesh."

The other members nodded, sagely.

"Things need to change," Stephanie continued, anger building in her voice. "We *must* believe in better for ourselves."

Another young woman who looked like Stephanie added, "Why do we want this? Because we hate and we want out. Nothing's fair, right? All we see is heartbreak, cruelty and injustice."

Patrick folded his arms across his chest, an affectionate smile stitched to his lips. "There is a better world," he said. "We know it. *Feel* it." His gaze drifted around the circle before finally focusing itself on Cameron. "Cameron, please introduce yourself. Tell us why you're here."

Cameron's cheeks burned. He sensed the group's eyes on him and stared at the palms of his hands for a moment. "I…I can't really pinpoint when and why things went wrong with Beth and I." He swallowed down a lump in his throat. "We were going through the motions, I guess. Safe in our habitual patterns and routines. Life was comfortable. Predictable, even.

"I first found out she was cheating on me when she accidentally left her laptop open. I think I knew, deep down, something wasn't right. That would explain why I trawled through her emails that day.

"I saw the messages – and that was the start of the end, really. She'd been living another life, searching for something that was missing from ours." He lowered his head, unable and unwilling to meet anyone's eyes.

"The divorce was messy. Poor Jess, our daughter. She was about to start her GCSEs, and of course her schooling suffered as a result. She hated Beth for what she'd done, for breaking up our family unit. I hated her, too. But that hate was tempered by guilt. Had I let her down as a husband?"

Beth momentarily appeared in his mind – red hair; freckles; that bright, pretty smile.

"I've always struggled to express my emotions. Beth said I was a closed book. When I found out she was cheating on me, my lack of reaction just concerned me into thinking I was more emotionally stunted than I thought."

He knitted his brows together as he carefully considered his next words.

"The court decided Beth would have Jess on weekends and I would have her during the week. Which was fine by me and Jess.

"Except… Jess's disdain for her mother never went away. And it came to the point where she didn't want to visit her mother at all."

Cameron closed his eyes, visualising his daughter's tear-streaked face in the darkness behind his lids.

"She was upset that Friday – the last time I saw her alive, I mean. She pleaded with me to let her stay home. Beth was living with another man, not even the same one she cheated on me with, in a house in Bristol.

"We sat in the car outside that house and Jess cried and cried. It was almost as though she *knew* something bad was going to happen. She usually got upset prior to me dropping her off, but never like this."

Cameron's voice sounded hoarse and hollow to his own ears.

"I reached out and shook her shoulder and told her everything was going to be fine, that she had to spend time with Beth because Beth had made plans for her... but secretly and selfishly I wanted her to go because I was craving a weekend alone, away from the responsibilities and pressures of being a parent."

The world seemed to be drifting from him, his body levitating from the moment. He blinked twice, rapidly, to dispel the notion. "I did love Jess. Loved her with all my heart. And when I think about the way she died..."

Screams. Smoke.

Panic.

Terror.

"She pleaded with me to take her back to my flat, but I told her to go. And I watched her walk sobbing, to that front door... and that was when I drove away." He clenched his hands, fingernails driving into the soft flesh of his palms.

"Then there was the fire. Beth's partner had fallen asleep with a cigarette in his hand and the whole house had gone up. Jess had been asleep in the spare bedroom at the time, and…"

He grabbed his face, breathing hard through his fingers. "I let her go into that house when she didn't want to. Now I have to live with that for the rest of my days."

Patrick leaned forward in his chair. "We're here to help. To listen. Remember – you're not alone."

The woman to Cameron's right, Megan, briefly touched his arm. "You *know*. You understand. You're one of us now." He could smell her perfume – something sweet and exotic – and found it oddly reassuring. He had no idea why.

When it was time to finish, Cameron helped the others pull the tables forward and stack the chairs.

"You will come back, won't you?" asked a middle-aged woman with thick red lipstick smeared around her mouth.

"You're not alone," reiterated a tall, nervous-looking man with glasses.

Cameron stepped out into the cold, then collapsed against a wall, sighing, shaking his head. He couldn't believe he'd opened up like that, in front of complete strangers, too. He heard a cough, and quickly turned. Patrick was outside, smoking a cigarette by a shattered telephone box. Inside the centre, Megan, Stephanie, and another blonde were

205

nattering away to each other in a corner. They appeared animated, kept glancing through the window at Cameron.

Patrick saw Cameron looking.

"My daughters." He waved at them and they waved back.

"All three?" Cameron asked.

"Yep." Patrick grimaced around his cigarette. "Can't imagine what you've been through. I'm so sorry, Cameron."

Cameron struggled to formulate a reply.

Patrick took one last puff on his cigarette, then flicked it away into the darkness. "When I was your age," he said, "I had no purpose. I drank too much, didn't look after myself at all. Like you, I was in a non-reciprocal relationship. We had the girls, but nothing in common." He rubbed his nose with the back of his hand. "Then, one day, I took them away." An odd laugh escaped him. "I got into trouble for that." He glanced at the Residents' Centre again. "But I knew best and in the end my girls came to me like moths to a light."

"You must be proud."

"I am." Patrick zipped his coat up. "There's still something left of Clara, though. Some small *sliver*. She clings to it, despite our…efforts."

Cameron was just about to ask what she was clinging to when the door opened behind him. He turned to see the three women emerge from the centre. They looked similar. Piercing grey eyes. Long blonde hair. The same high cheekbones and thin, crooked mouth.

"Good to meet you." Patrick stuck out his hand. Cameron shook it. "Will you be back? We'd very much like it, Cameron."

Cameron forced a smile. "Sure."

He was dimly aware of the women whispering to each other as he left the premises. He rounded a corner by the convenience store, hurried along Rodden Road. Streetlamps painted terraces, cars slithered past him. A group of youths in hoodies shared a bottle of cider on the corner of Beechwood Avenue.

He crossed the street, then wheeled when he heard his name being called.

One of the women was racing after him, frantically waving her arms.

Megan.

"Sorry," she said, reaching him, panting. She quickly got her breath back. "Didn't mean to startle you."

"You didn't. You okay?"

She tugged at the collar of her blouse. "I feel...*silly*."

"Why?"

"It's just..." Her arms fell limply to her sides. "I hope you don't think me forward. I've always been spontaneous, and..." She rolled her eyes. "God, I'm rambling here, aren't I?" She laughed, shrilly. Then, clearing her throat, composing herself, she said: "You're not like the others. I mean, the people who usually come through our door. I knew it as soon as I set eyes on you."

Her lips formed a coy smile. "I find you attractive. There. Said it."

207

He stared at her.

That smile. The piercing eyes. The smell of her perfume.

It awakened something inside him that he thought was long dead.

April, 2014

They emerged from the cinema, their eyes struggling to adapt to the daylight. Cork Street was busy, bustling and squirming with shoppers.

"Well, that was...odd." Cameron buttoned his coat up.

Megan's heels clacked on the concrete beside him. "Very," she agreed.

Cameron's head was filled with black rooms, dark pools and weird forests. He'd appreciated the passive air Scarlett Johansson had exuded, but the film itself had been unsettling and strange.

"I didn't like it." Megan hitched her handbag up over her shoulder. "It was such a cold experience."

"Think that was the whole point of it."

"But that's how I feel about *all* films." He looked at her, and her sad smile told him she was being serious. "Same for music and books. I don't get them, Cam."

"You don't get them?" He laughed warily, shaking his head from side-to-side. "It's going to be tough thinking up tdate ideas with you."

She shrugged. "I'm just happy to be with you, that's all."

They resumed walking, a taut silence stretching between them. Suddenly feeling the need to talk, Cameron said, "You honestly don't like films? Going to the cinema was a weekly highlight for me when I was a kid."

"There's nothing these things can ever teach me, because there's only The Way."

There it is again, he thought, turning his face away before she could say anything more.

She gripped his arm, pulling him back to her. "Sorry, I'm sorry." She clawed a hand through her hair. "I'm not much fun, am I? It's just... I want to be with you. And I'm desperate to show you what *I've* experienced. What I've seen. There's no room in my head for anything else. But if I can share it..."

"Show me, then."

Her face brightened. She nodded and they linked arms and pushed on, through the crowd. "Emotions are dumb things. They enslave us, make us weak."

"What about the flip side? Don't you ever feel good about yourself?"

She chewed her lip. "Only when I'm around you," she replied.

They arrived at the flat just as it was getting dark. Cameron let them in with his key. He closed the door behind them, thoughts festering in his mind.

Was it the right time to broach Shining Way? To finally get his feelings off his chest? There was so much he wasn't sure about, not least the way *they* were controlling Megan.

209

A cork popped. Megan stepped out of the kitchen holding two glasses of bubbly. They sat on the settee and stretched their legs out. Headlamps from the traffic outside swept through the room.

Megan touched his face.

Say something, he thought. But she spoke before he could. "Got something for you."

"Oh?"

She nodded at the coffee table.

There was a brown envelope on it, partially hidden by a TV-listings magazine. "Open it."

He scooped up and tore open the envelope, extracting the printouts inside. He scanned them, realising it was confirmation bookings for a ferry to Bilbao and a hotel room in Rennes-le-Château for six nights.

She flung her arms around his neck, laughing, nibbling his ear. He couldn't ruin this moment by expressing doubt; he knew she'd get upset with him. He'd have to go along with it, see what she wanted him to see. Which meant having to abandon their little chat about Shining Way for now.

She took the paperwork from him and put it back on the coffee table. "Dad bought it for us."

Of course, Cameron thought. *Patrick. Who else?*

"Stay there." She jumped up and headed for the kitchen, returning moments later with the champagne bottle. She topped them both up. "To France," she said, their glasses chinking together.

"To France."

She put the bottle down on the floor. Snuggled into him and played with his hair. She'd want to go to bed soon.

She drew back suddenly, her eyes tight and worried looking. "You're very quiet."

"Been thinking about my dreams again."

"What've you been dreaming this time?"

"Don't know," he shrugged. "Don't tend to remember much about them, to be honest. Just the feelings they leave behind, I guess." His mouth managed to shape itself into a smile. "I tend to wake up... *exhausted* from them."

She touched his face softly, deftly, then dropped her hand onto the settee. "You know I can manipulate dreams, don't you?" She let out a small, playful giggle. "With my magic rays, I can erase thoughts and memories. You're under my spell, Cam. Under my complete control and command."

He stared at her for a long moment. Then, quietly chuckling to himself, he pulled her in close, drawing in the scent of her perfume, her hair. "You're a strange one," he said. "Scarlett Johansson's got nothing on you."

211

Part II

"When the time comes, we'll shine like stars.
"The world doesn't owe us a thing, remember?
"Sear it away. Sear it all away.
"Let's burn it down and start again."

July, 2014

Megan and Cameron picnicked in a small, pretty village a mile or so north of Rennes-le-Château. There was some sort of festival going on, the streets decked out with banners, streamers and flags. They sat in the heart of the village, on a bench in the shade, eating crepes and ice-cream from white plastic bowls.

Enthusiastic French voices burst from Tannoy speakers lashed to streetlamps, the language barrier reminding Cameron of the funeral and how, during his eulogy, he had struggled to convey his loss.

He put his bowl down, watching Megan's hand creep across the bench toward him. Taking his hand, she weaved her fingers between his and squeezed.

"I was thinking about Jess," he said, hunching up so that she couldn't see his face. "What I'd do to see her again, Meg."

Megan was quiet, like he knew she would be.

People moved about them, carrying hotdogs and plastic cups filled with beer. Birds chattered from telegraph wires, litter skipped and danced about their feet. Finally, Cameron met her gaze.

Her eyes were cold, hard, and unblinking.

"What was one of the first things I taught you?" She wormed her hand free of his, dropping it behind her back. "The world's not fair, life's not fair. It's what we're fighting against, right?" She puffed out her cheeks. "All we have is the belief there's a better world."

He nodded absently, his thoughts wandering.

Megan, Shining Way, The Light – what did it all mean? These days, he was too scared to contemplate, too afraid to think where they might take him. "We've got each other," he said.

His cheeks coloured when she laughed and he looked down to hide his embarrassment.

She lowered her head to make him see her, a pitying smile creeping across her face. "You're a sweetheart, you know that? One of the good ones." The smile vanished and she glared almost conspiratorially around them. "You talk about you and me and it's beautiful, Cam, it really is. But things'll be *different* soon. Us, together... that's *selfish* talk." She gripped his arm, fingernails digging into his flesh. "There's a change coming. I know you don't understand." That smile snaked across her face again. "You will."

She got up and walked away before he could reply. He found his feet, following her toward a cluster of rickety, decrepit-looking buildings. His mind was racing, his thoughts muddled by the intense heat and humidity. Megan was changing, taking control of his world once more.

They found a small, ivy-clad church at the bottom of a lane. There was no door, just a black

213

square in the wall, like an entrance to a cave. Megan stooped, disappearing into darkness. Cameron, palming sweat from off his face, followed her inside.

Cool air enveloped him, a welcome respite from the stifling heat. His gaze focused, picking out stone effigies of saint-like figures, their hands pressed together, their eyes painted a gaudy silver. Candle flames wavered in shallow, shadowy alcoves. A stained-glass window set in the farthest wall depicted an image of a man with rays of light shooting from his mouth and eyes.

There were three murals dressing the wall opposite. Cameron squinted and stared, quickly ascertaining what each one represented.

The first depicted the Israelites carrying the Ark of the Covenant through a desert, toward the banks of the River Jordan, the Ark hidden beneath a veil made of skins and blue cloth.

The second showed King David bringing the Ark to Jerusalem.

The third depicted the Virgin Mary with her arms stretched out in benediction, her wide eyes shining like stars.

A hand shot out, seizing his arm.

He turned to see an elderly man in robes and a clerical collar, his countenance a road-map of lines, scars, and wrinkles.

"Soldat." The old priest grinned, specks of light dancing in his rheumy eyes. "*Soldat*."

Cameron broke away, hurrying to Megan's side. She was staring at dozens of photographs pinned above an altar in the corner. Dust whirled in

214

the half-lit space between them, forming and re-forming new worlds. "Meg?"

She blinked and smiled at him. "Look," she said, pointing excitedly. Cameron looked at the photos, noting they all depicted the same crumbling chapel by the side of a long and deserted country road. "*Lieu de lumière*." A dreamy smile passed across her face.

He grabbed hold of her arm. "Can we go now, please?"

They stepped back out into the raging sunshine. Cameron's senses felt flooded, laughter from a group of tourists serving only to heighten his disorientation.

"The priest." He paced the spot, rubbing his brow with his fingers. "That priest in the church… He said something to me just now."

Megan gave a cryptic little smile. "He called you 'soldier'." He stared blankly at her. "Let's go in here."

She led him by the hand through a rust-eaten gate into a small, neglected churchyard. They sat on a bench in the shade, staring at ancient headstones and crosses slicing out of the overgrowth.

"Why are we here?" Cameron wiped his sleeve across his forehead.

"You'll see." She twirled a long length of her hair with her fingers until one by one the strands slipped from her grasp. "It's the final jump of the hoop. An initiation. A pilgrimage, if you like."

He grimaced, sweat trickling down the length of his face.

215

"Hey," she said, nudging him. "Let's go out for dinner tonight." Her pale lips twitched into a grin. "Then I can reveal to you why we're here. The *real* reason, Cam."

March, 2014

Just before 7PM, Cameron arrived at the Residents' Centre for another group meet-up. The same old faces were there – Patrick and his three daughters, Stephanie, Clara, and Megan. The two other regular attendees were absent, no new faces had come through the door for weeks.

Cameron took off his jacket, folding it over the back of a chair. Megan was seated beside him, rocking from side-to-side, a spaced-out smile all over her face. He shook her arm gently, tenderly, but she didn't react to him at all.

He'd seen her like this before. The first time he thought she was on something. Patrick had to take him to one side and explain it was a form of meditation – of 'tuning in' to the light.

Under her breath she was whispering something, the words uttered in a quiet, sing-song voice. *"Light through the veins, light through the veins..."*

Patrick and Stephanie were smiling, but Clara was locked inside herself, tugging at her hair, staring down at the floor at nothing.

Patrick sermonised for a while, revealing: "The things we see! The stuff we *dream*. It's mind-blowing, Cameron, it really is." Under the fluorescent glare of the strip-lights, his smile looked vaguely grotesque. "You're here because you want it, too."

No, Cameron thought. *I'm here for Megan. She brought me back from the dead. Got me to think and feel again. I'm not interested in your bullshit, whatever it is you believe in. The only thing I believe in is Meg.*

Suddenly, Clara spoke; spinning in her seat, she shrieked at Cameron – "Don't think she cares! All this *empathy* and understanding is –"

"Enough!" Patrick was quickly on his feet, bending at the waist, whispering to Clara: "What's got into you? You need to stop this – *now*."

Silence.

Megan flopped back into her seat, a wry smile stitched to her lips. Stephanie averted her gaze to the wall.

Should Cameron say something? Ask what this was about? He opened his mouth, but thought better of it. This had nothing to do with him. He felt temporarily locked out. Lost.

Clara got to her feet, then made her way to the storeroom, slamming the door shut behind her. Megan rocked forwards, turning her face away as she sniggered into her hands. Patrick and Stephanie took their coffee mugs over to the sink to wash up. Their collective silence felt awkward and tense.

Cameron turned to Megan. "You coming to mine tonight?"

"No," she whispered. "Not tonight. I'm staying with my sisters this evening."

217

He shot up from his seat, approaching Patrick and Stephanie over by the sink. Megan resumed chanting and singing behind him.

Patrick frowned. "You okay, Cameron?"

"Just thinking about leaving. It's a long walk home for me."

"Sorry about Clara." Patrick put a hand on his shoulder. "She gets like that sometimes. Jealousy, I think. She's always wanted what her sisters have got. It's not her fault, not really. She *was* the last to go in."

Cameron raised his eyebrows in puzzlement. "The last to go in?"

"By then I expect the power had diminished somewhat. We'll take her back someday."

"You've lost me."

Patrick nodded at Megan. "We'll look after her tonight, Cameron."

Cameron turned to face Megan again.

Her eyelids were fluttering in perfect synchronicity with the flickering of the strip-light above her head.

He left them then. Walked out of the building and into the night. A waft of fried food and grease from the chip shop filled his nostrils. Car headlamps washed across the pavement. Kids laughing in a shop doorway helped anchor him to the world, establishing a sense of normality again.

Both Megan and Clara's behaviour had greatly disturbed him tonight. *Don't think she cares!* Christ, what had Clara *meant* by that? Perhaps Patrick was right and it had all been a simple display of jealously on her part.

218

Cameron stopped abruptly, rubbing his arms and shivering. He'd left his jacket behind. If he was quick enough, he could run up and get it.

He jogged back onto St. John's Road, passing the convenience store and chip shop. Perhaps Megan would change her mind and come on home with him, he thought, hopefully.

He arrived back at the centre. Clara was still sitting on her chair, sobbing her heart out. Patrick was crouched beside her, whispering: "…only The Light remains." Stephanie was standing over them and all three looked up and around as he entered.

He felt like he was intruding and immediately blushed. "Sorry. Forgot my jacket."

"It's all right, Cameron." Patrick straightened up and smiled at him.

Cameron hurried to his chair, scooped up his jacket. Patrick was staring at him with no discernible expression on his face at all. "Where's Megan?"

"She's in the storeroom." Patrick clasped his hands together in front of him, rocking backwards and forwards on his heels. "She's very tired."

Cameron approached the back door. "I didn't say goodbye. I'll just…"

"No. She's fine. Leave her."

Was there a hint of panic to his voice?

"Two minutes."

Patrick stepped forward to intercept, but Cameron was already opening and moving through the back door. He slipped into a small, square corridor. To his right, the entrance to the toilet; to his left, the storeroom's grey, unpainted door.

219

He twisted its handle, pushing at the same time.

The lights were off. Toys and play apparatus were lurking mounds of shadow. Over in the corner, Megan was standing in front of the window, her hands spread out against the glass.

"Meg?"

He froze, then put his hand over his mouth.

Her eyes were glowing, *shining*, painting that small section of the room with light. As she whispered to herself, scores of moths fluttered and flickered beyond the pane.

He closed the door on her, breathing deep, trying to compose himself. Then, swiftly shaking his head, he wheeled and returned to the centre's main room.

Patrick and Stephanie looked around at him. They were over by the sink again. Cameron crossed the room, pushing through the front door. He saw Clara outside, lingering beside the vandalised telephone box.

"I saw Meg," he told her, his voice shaky, faint. "Her eyes… The moths…"

Clara stepped forward, her face looking pale and fraught in the darkness.

"Ever wondered why moths stay at lights?" she asked. Cameron could only shake his head in reply. "A moth's eyes have sensors. They adjust according to the amount of light they detect." Her face glittered brightly with tears. "A moth's dark-adapting mechanism responds slower than its light-adapting mechanism. So, once the moth comes to a light, it finds it difficult to return…to the dark, I mean. They're blind for ages. They can't pull

220

themselves away." She cupped her hand over her mouth, then took it away again. "Neither will you."

July, 2014

The sun was sinking, the sky a dark, smouldering violet. Stars glinted behind rows of inanimate cypress trees. They sat in the outside area of a restaurant, under a green plastic canopy. Megan ordered mussels, Cameron an omelette. As they waited for their meals, Megan checked the GPS on her phone. "Not far now." She put the phone back down on the table and smiled at him.

The smile vanished. "What's wrong, Cam?"

Cameron was on the verge of full-blown panic. Something was screaming for him to leave; to abandon Megan and this weird pilgrimage immediately.

He abruptly stood.

"Where are you going?"

"The rest room." He pushed his chair in. "Won't be long."

He stumbled to the back of the restaurant, along a crumbling path strewn with weeds. The trees bowed over a low wall, thin and skeletal in the gloaming. He reached the outhouse, pushed through the door. Staggered to a slime-encrusted basin and vomited, violently, into it. Seconds later, he lifted his head. A cracked mirror above the sink distorted his features, pulling his eyes askew.

He twisted a tap, cupped his hands under it. Splashed cold water onto his face. Soon, the nausea passed. He straightened, wiping vomit away from

221

his mouth. "You're okay," he whispered. "It'll all be okay."

He could slip away without her noticing. Just climb the wall, walk out across the fields and leave; it was as simple as that. Instead, he placed a hand on the basin and squeezed shut his eyes.

Where are you?

He was finding it increasingly hard to visualise his daughter's face now. Why couldn't he picture it anymore? Why wasn't it there?

"You okay?" Megan asked as soon as he returned to their table.

He sat back down in his seat. "Sure."

The waiter arrived before she could say anything more, putting their plates of food down in front of them. Megan pushed her mobile into her pocket, tucked a loose strand of hair behind her ear.

Later, as they ate, he asked, "So, what is it we're looking for?"

222

Part III

"Don't look at me.

"I don't want you to see me like this. You're not ready. You wouldn't understand.

"Sleep. Go back to your dreams. They'll prepare you for the searing."

June, 2014

"DAD!"

Jess.

Oh, shit.

Jess.

He gripped the handrail, bounding up the stairs, smoke surrounding him in a thick cocoon of floating embers and scorching ash. He had to keep going – couldn't stop now.

Three-quarters of the way up, he spotted Jess through the smoke. He braced himself, then plunged through the flames, coughing, spluttering, reaching. Heat blasted. Fire seared. He gripped Jess's shoulder, turned her to him. "Got you," he gasped. "Got you, thank God."

It wasn't Jess.

Megan was standing there instead, grinning at him.

He stumbled backwards, disorientated. As the smoke withdrew, he realised they weren't in a house at all, but his flat, his sitting room. He dropped his hands to his sides and stared at her, then looked helplessly around.

He was just about to ask where Jess was when Megan said, quietly, "Come and look," and led him by the hand over to the window.

The sky was on fire.

It looked like it was about to fall and burn the city to a cinder at any given moment.

She tossed her head back and laughed, loudly.

"Wonderful," she said. "Isn't it?"

May, 2014

"…and it works kind of like a battery. It needs time to charge. It's an amazing…"

Megan was leaning over him, whispering softly, her fingers lightly brushing his face.

His eyelids cracked open.

"Morning," she smiled.

He sat up, the bed creaking beneath him. "What was that?" he said, kneading his eyes with his fists. "What were you saying just then?"

"You were dreaming," she replied.

"Christ," he said, shaking his head from side-to-side, "think I'm more tired now than I was when I went to bed."

"Seven more weeks," she giggled.

He pushed her aside and quickly clambered out of bed.

"What shall we do today?" she asked him.

"I should start looking for a job." He grabbed some fresh jeans and a T-shirt. "Start contributing to society again."

He knew she wouldn't like that.

Perhaps it was her rant yesterday about the news on TV that had darkened his mood, but right now he was finding it hard just to talk to her.

"Why?" She flicked her hair out of her eyes. "We've enough money to get by on. We don't need much."

"I'm stagnating."

"All the better to get away, then." She breathed out an exasperated sigh. "Everything will seem so much clearer after our break, Cam."

He pulled on his clothes, throwing a guilty glance back at her. "I don't want to go."

There, he thought. *Said it.* She winced and sat up, a swift shadow of anger sweeping across her face. "Then you'll be denying yourself!" she hissed. "If you want to be a sad little nobody, then that's your business. You'll come and go like the rest of them." Her cheekbones twitched, her eyes blazed. "Don't you want to be part of something *better?* Part of something different, amazing, and... *eternal?*"

He took a deep breath before saying, "That's the problem. You keep me in the dark all the time. You never let me in on what's going on." His voice cracked. He swiftly rubbed his eyes to stem the tears.

She kicked off the duvet and rushed across the room to him, flinging her arms around his neck. "When are you going to realise you're looking at this the wrong way?" she cried. "You've got yourself all worked up, haven't you? You need to view it from a different angle – see the bigger picture! I can't help you anymore, not until we're *there.*" She drew back, looking him straight in the eye. "You're doing this for me, remember? Because you're a lovely man. Because you like me. And I like you. You don't have to be alone anymore." She hardened her voice. "Never lose sight of your hate. Shape your pain and despair into a weapon of *truth*. We've a message to send, and the world needs to hear it, Cam."

July, 2014

"Shouldn't we be going back to the hotel?" Cameron glanced round at Megan as she drove them along a deserted country road. They passed dark fields, dilapidated barns and black, shapeless farmhouses. "It's getting late."

"Not yet," she replied, flashing him a peculiar half-smile.

Just outside of Rennes-le-Château, she flicked the indicator stem and pulled up into a layby. She cranked the handbrake, nodding out of the window at a chapel on the other side of the road. "Go in there," she said. "*Please,* Cam."

He couldn't drag his gaze away from her face. "The chapel?" He emitted a quiet, uneasy sounding laugh. "That's the one in the photographs. The ones in the church we visited, right?"

"Please. No questions. Just go inside."

He sighed, nodded his head and opened the front passenger door, reluctantly sliding himself out of the vehicle.

The moon glowed over the chapel's steeply pitched roof. Crickets sang. Stars glinted between the knotted branches of a dead yew.

He crossed the road, opened an iron gate and edged down a path to the chapel's arched wooden door. Pinned or placed on a ledge above the entrance were photographs, colourful-looking beads, silver lockets and strands of hair in small, polythene bags.

Carved into the wood of the door were the words *Lieu de lumière*.

"Power distilled from the Ark and then contained within walls."

Several threads of thought churned and tossed themselves inside his mind.

Taking all he'd heard and learnt into consideration, this place had the potential to change him. He was already broken; what else did he have to lose?

He closed his eyes, searching for Jess in the darkness behind his lids. But again, her face was too indistinct, the features hazy and ill-defined.

With my magic rays, I can erase thoughts and memories.

He reopened his eyes. Grit his teeth and pushed through the chapel's door.

The moon spread its light onto an altar covered by a blue sheet with white stars and hook-shaped moons patterned across it. There was a small table and a chair in front of the altar. A cracked statue of a saint lurked in one corner, its pale hands clasped together, its eyes painted a gaudy silver.

The air crackled with unnatural energy, causing the hairs on the back of his neck to stand on end.

Pilgrimage.

Initiation.

Baptism.

Those words exploded like fireworks inside his skull.

He didn't have to be here. It wasn't too late to turn back. But without Jess and Beth, what did he have?

"Megan," he whispered.

Megan.

Perhaps he really was under her control. Maybe he was being used. But she was all he had now; there was nobody else for him in this world.

He closed the door, then groped for the chair and sat. His breath came in thick, strangled rasps. His heart thudded and thundered. Something, he sensed, was in the room with him, slowly beginning to form, to manifest – wanting to replace so much of him with itself.

The darkness cracked right open, arrows of bright, blinding, pure, white light suddenly shooting out and striking him a dozen times in quick succession.

He was knocked to his feet, a shrill noise ringing in his ears; it took a moment or two for him to realise it was the sound of his own screaming.

He found and flung open the door. Megan was stood outside, waiting for him by the iron gate. She moved quickly to him, taking hold of his arm, helping him across the road. She opened the Clio's doors, sitting him down and securing his seatbelt.

He was sweating profusely, burning up and shivering.

She leapt into the driver's seat and drove quickly away, the markings in the road soon flashing and skipping beneath them again.

She glanced at him. Bit down hard on her lip before refocusing on the road.

"We came along this way," she said, "after Mum left Dad. Dad – Patrick – took us here without Mum knowing. He wanted to take us away from all that was false... all that was *weak*." She gripped the wheel with both hands until her knuckles whitened. "We stopped there, at that place. Dad went in first. Then we all did – me; my sisters, Steph and Clara."

She pulled in a sharp breath. "That place... it spoke to us. To *all* of us... to varying degrees." Cameron thought of Clara. *There's still something left. Some small* sliver.

Megan fell silent again. The markings continued to skip and flash under them. Cameron couldn't speak, couldn't even bring himself to look at her. He lifted his head and saw his eyes were shining from his reflection in the windscreen.

"You've been there." Megan's frail voice trembled. "You've experienced it. It's *good*... right?"

Cameron slunk down in his seat and, covering his face with his hands, wept and sobbed until only The Light remained.

229

Highways

I met Lara in *The Cellar* – a dark, cavernous bar under Welch Road. As our eyes locked from across the room, I thought it had been a long time since I'd seen anyone so devastatingly attractive. Her thin, almost porcelain face was perfectly framed by long dark hair. She wore a grey Nirvana "Smiley" T-shirt and ripped denim jeans.

It took all my courage to approach her, but I needn't have worried; Lara was warm, open, funny. Turned out we'd both attended the same primary school. We also shared an enthusiasm for Nick Cave records and Elmore Leonard novels.

"So," she picked a strand of hair away from her eyes, "what do you do?"

"I'm a wound care specialist for a medical company," I replied. "Nothing exciting. You?"

Lara was a hairdresser. She owned a salon in Alverstoke Village and was doing extremely well for herself. "It's all starting to come together, you know? Like I've finally found my place in the world."

We talked for over an hour, perched together on a hard bench in an alcove at the back of the bar. Posters for clubs and rock bands plastered the walls around us. It felt like our own dark cosmos: we were so utterly, so perfectly alone there.

At the end of the evening, I peeled the label off a beer bottle and scribbled my number on the back of it. "Here," I said, passing it to her. "I'd really like to do this again sometime."

A smile spilled across her face.

It made me feel like we were the only two people in the world.

In the market along High Street, I bought a glass-framed picture of Route 101. This was on the same day that Lara moved in with me. Route 101 is now, of course, the famous Hollywood Freeway. It's the road where Norma Jean Baker posed for one of her first photo shoots shortly before her reincarnation as Marilyn Monroe. I've always been obsessed with long, dusty desert highways. I dream of driving from Los Angeles into the Nevada Desert in one of those old convertible Cadillacs. It's a faded postcard dream I know, but I like to look at it once in a while.

I took the picture back to my apartment and hung it over our bed. Like the view of the sea through my window, it reminded me that nobody's ever really tied to anything.

"I want to travel," I told Lara as I hammered a nail in the wall. "I don't want to stay in this depressing corner of England my whole life."

Lara went quiet on me. She moved toward the window, gazing out at the black waves crashing and disintegrating around the Isle of Wight.

"But I've got everything I want here," she said. "My shop, my family. I couldn't even imagine leaving."

A year passed. Lara's business was going great guns; to cope with the demand, she had to employ a couple of students from St. Vincent's College. But I'd grown bored with my own job. I was anxious to do something else, to escape the nine-to-five day.

Lara knew I wanted to move from Gosport, and it put a serious strain on our relationship.

One afternoon, it came to a head.

"It feels like we're pulling in opposite directions," she said, a note of desperation in her voice. "I'm going to stay at Mum's for a while, Dan. I think we both need some space; some time alone."

I watched her speed off in her Fiesta, then let the front room curtain flap back into place.

I decided to take a walk outside, to get some air, to try and clear my head of clutter. It was bitter cold out, snow swirling down from the sky to settle on the pavements and roads. I ended up by Alver creek. Dilapidated fishing boats sliced out of the mire. As my eyes roamed the mud, litter and debris, I saw something odd – something *impossible* – under Alver Bridge.

I scaled the railings, dropping down into the darkness of the embankment. I trudged through thick mud, wastepaper blowing about my ankles. I ducked beneath the bridge, tilting my head to one side as I studied it.

The hole was about six inches in length, maybe an inch or two wide. I pushed my finger into it, making it real. My finger lost all sensation, turning cold and dead. I drew it out quickly, shivered, then turned away, hurrying out from under the bridge toward the normality of the town centre.

Night was falling by the time I arrived home. My apartment accreted darkness in layers, like earth heaped onto a grave.

Just before ten, the telephone rang.

"We need to talk."

Lara.

"Yeah. I know."

"Pick me up from work tomorrow. Don't be late."

I put the phone down, and immediately there was a power cut. Everything went – lights, TV, clock. It only lasted a few seconds. But the silence, coupled with the claustrophobic darkness, felt terrifying.

***

Lara worked quickly as snow pattered against the window, nattering away to the woman in the chair about last night's episode of *Friends*.

I felt a twinge of irritation.

After her last customer left, Lara locked up the salon and I drove us home. Streetlights cast our white faces onto the darkness of the windscreen.

"Human nature fascinates me," she said, having sensed my irritation back at the shop. "I want to know about people, Dan. Is that so bad?"

Back home, the apartment felt colder than usual. I closed the door, kicked off my shoes. Lara switched on the TV.

"I thought we were going to talk," I said.

"Too tired. Let's leave it until tomorrow."

I drifted over to the window, planting the flats of my hands against the glass. "I'm going for a walk then," I replied.

Outside, the snow had stopped. A brittle slice of moon emitted a cold light, fluorescently harsh,

233

guiding me toward the creek. I kept telling myself that what I had seen the other day hadn't been real.

The river reeked of tar, salt, and mud. I glanced up and down the street, then carefully scaled the railings.

Despite the night you could still see it.

I wrapped my coat around me, trying to make sense of it all over again.

"What does it mean?"

I wheeled.

A teenager was stood on the bank, next to a discarded fridge. His face was drenched in cold, cold moonlight.

"I don't know," I whispered, turning to it again.

That was when I noticed the crowd, congregating on the towpath above, staring down at the bridge with eyes as black and empty as the hole.

***

The next day there was a quiet, almost subdued air to the office. I surfed the Internet and looked at websites on travel and tourism, just to relieve the boredom. I gazed at pictures of Highway 101 and the US 50 before downloading a Route 66 screensaver.

In the afternoon, I had to train up a new girl called Claire. She sat with me as I showed her how to use our computer system. She talked. I didn't.

"I've just finished a three-year Economics degree at Southampton University," she told me as we waited for the computer to warm up. "It's weird

234

how your life can change at the drop of a hat. I dumped my boyfriend on the day of my graduation. We'd been going out together for four years – well, on and off, anyway. Now, I feel great. It's good to be free of him. God, does that sound callous?"

I shrugged, shaking my head.

"Now I know who I am, and what I can achieve with my life. The world's exciting again, like it is when you're a child."

She laughed.

Whenever the light fell into her eyes, it was like somebody dropping a stone into a pool. Highways formed and reformed; roads more exotic and dangerous than any I'd seen before.

Later, she said: "I moved from Southampton to start afresh. I don't know this area at all. Perhaps you could show me around? I'd like to know where the best clubs and bars are."

She smiled at me from behind her hair. I wondered how much she meant by that.

I was home by six. As I snapped the kitchen light on, I saw the note from Lara tacked to the refrigerator. *Staying at Mum's tonight. See you soon. L.*

***

"You should stop trying to cling to one another," Darren said, leaning back in his chair. "It's obviously doing more harm than good."

Darren was a mate of mine – we'd worked together in the dockyards a few years back. We were at his favourite haunt, *Nelson's*, a dingy pub located on the corner of High Street.

"We're at that stage where we're too frightened to cement what we've got," I said, "and too afraid to break up. It's like we're stuck in some kind of vacuum."

I remembered something Lara had once said – *"Even if we'd been born at opposite ends of the Earth, we'd still have found each other. Our roads would have crossed somehow."*

Darren's eyes were bloodshot. "You okay?" I asked, leaning across the table.

He shrugged. "I'm not sleeping. But it's no different for anyone else. People are retreating, hiding inside themselves. And it's not just because of this weather."

I glanced across at the window. High Street was deserted. Litter and dead leaves flapped against the steps of the old Methodist church.

"Weird how quiet everything is," I whispered.

Darren wasn't listening. He was huddled over the table, staring into his pint.

I left my seat and walked over to the bar. As I searched my pockets for change, a crowd of people passed by the window. Their voices seemed to bring the night alive. Darren stood up suddenly, knocking his chair to the floor. "Come on," he said, wrestling into his coat. "If we're quick enough, we can catch them."

It had started snowing again. Flakes dusted the roads, moonlight drenched the terraces. At the base of each house was its own crooked shadow.

We followed the crowd through a maze of streets. There were more people near the river, standing around in gangs, or sitting beside small makeshift fires. Most had found a space on the bank or under the bridge itself, but there were also figures loitering on the road above, their outlines sketched out by the streetlights.

"Must be hundreds of us," I breathed.

Darren wasn't listening. He jolted into life, clambered quickly over the railings, dropped like a stone into darkness. Then, from under the bridge, people began to raise their voices in song. Candle flames flickered in the darkness like tongues.

An elderly man at my elbow said: "It's bigger now. It's getting bigger all the time. Reckon soon they'll be able to fit a person through it. And then what?"

***

I woke the next morning with a start, blinking, groaning, tossing back the covers and heading straight for the window. I pulled back the curtain and gazed in disbelief at the world outside.

I anxiously touched the window, hoping and praying it was just the glass that was cracked and not the sky.

I sat down on the edge of the bed, gripping my knees, wondering if it was worth going to work. Oddly, I thought of Claire. I wondered if she would be in today.

Even if we'd been born at opposite ends of the Earth, we'd still have found each other.

I left my apartment and wandered the streets, unnerved by the dereliction and silence. The remains of snow salted car windscreens and rooftops. I walked along a deserted Welch Road, then took the iron staircase down to *The Cellar*. The bar seemed even darker than usual.

I drifted over to an alcove, and a pale face peeled itself from the darkness.

"Funny how well we know each other." Lara scraped a strand of hair away from her eyes. She was sat on our bench, sipping a large glass of red wine.

I took my coat off and folded it over the back of a chair. I wanted to ask her why she wasn't with everybody else. Instead, I asked: "Has it really been two and a half years since we first met here? I remembered thinking, *there's nowhere else I want to be.*"

I reached out and touched her face. "Why doesn't anybody *talk* about it?" she whispered, smoothing the rim of her glass.

"Do you want another drink?"

"No. Thanks. But help yourself, Dan, there's no one here. Take whatever you want."

I sidled behind the bar, grabbed a tumbler and helped myself to the scotch. "We did see it," she called out. "I mean, we're not going to fool each other over that, right? Because there's no point in *not* talking about it."

I glanced at her. She reached out across the table for her cigarettes, her pretty dark eyes not leaving my face.

"They've found other tears, holes, whatever you want to call them. In London, in Manchester. Places abroad. They're turning up *everywhere*. There's a large tear in Giza, near the Pyramids. People are flocking to them in their thousands." Her voice trembled. "Did you *see* the sky this morning?"

"Yes," I said.

"What's going on out there, Dan?"

I sat down next to her. Lara put her head on my shoulder. "Everyone's going or gone," she whispered. "There's no one."

Beyond our alcove, beyond our cosmos, the darkness thickened. I couldn't tell whether it was the dark or just... nothingness.

"I'm here," I said, after a pause. "I'm beside you. Even if there's no one else, it doesn't matter."

I pulled her close to me and felt her tears on my skin, so warm and silent.

Then we held each other for what seemed like forever, too afraid to let go.

Acknowledgements

Many thanks to the following who originally
published these stories:

Adrian Chamberlin, Peter Coleborn, Dorothy
Davies, Trevor Denyer, Dean M Drinkel, Paul
Finch, Terry Grimwood, Stuart Hughes and Steve
Lines.

ABOUT THE AUTHOR

Paul Edwards was born and raised in Bristol, UK, and now lives in the Somerset town of Frome. He has been published in anthologies such as *Darker Battlefields, The Darkest Battlefield, Terror Tales of Cornwall, Something Remains, A Feast of Frights* and *Dark Doorways*. He is a fan of rock music, rough cider and horror movies. He's currently hard at work on his first novel.

You can contact Paul at
pauledwards1976@hotmail.com

pauledwardswriter.wordpress.com